T0108276

# THIS WAR
# CALLED LOVE

# THIS WAR
# CALLED LOVE

Nine Stories

by Alejandro Murguía

City Lights Books

San Francisco

Copyright © 2002 by Alejandro Murguía

All Rights Reserved

Cover Design: Amy Trachtenberg and Robin Raschke
Book design: Small World Productions

The following stories first appeared in slightly different form:
"A Toda Máquina" in *Dorothy Parker's Elbow: Tattoos on Writers,
Writers on Tattoos*. Edited by Kim Addonizio and Cheryl Dumesnil.
Warner Books, 2002. "Rose-Colored Dreams" in *Chelsea*, no. 64,
April 1998, and *San Francisco Focus Magazine*, December 1994, and
(as "Selling Flowers on Mission Street") in *Oxygen*, no. 6, 1992.
"A Lesson in Merengue" in *Latin Style Magazine*, Los Angeles, vol. l,
no. 5, 1995. "El Último Round" in *The San Francisco Bay Guardian*,
San Francisco, May, 1995. "Lucky Alley" in *Currents from the
Dancing River*. Edited by Ray Gonzalez, Harcourt Brace, 1994.

Library of Congress Cataloging-in-Publication Data

Murguía, Alejandro, 1949-
      This war called love : nine stories/by Alejandro Murguía
            p. cm.
Contents: Boy on a wooden horse—El último round—Ofrendas—
The flower seller—Barrio lotto—Lucky Alley—A lesson in
merengue—A toda máquina—This war called love.

ISBN 0-87286-394-8
      1. United States—Social Life and customs—20th century—
Fiction. 2. Mexico—Social life and customs—Fiction. 3. Hispanic
American men—Fiction. 4. Mexican Americans—Fiction. I. Title

PS3563.U7255 T48 2002
813'.54—dc21

                                             2002020888

CITY LIGHTS BOOKS are edited by Lawrence Ferlinghetti and
Nancy J. Peters and published at the City Lights Bookstore,
261 Columbus Avenue, San Francisco CA 94133.

www.citylights.com

## Acknowledgments

The author thanks the gente of La Mission, San Pancho, whose empowering spirit carried me through the lean times when my life had no art and no stories. Nancy J. Peters at City Lights who took the chance. Los vatos de aquellas—Roberto Vargas and raúlrsalinas in Tejas; Anuar Murrar along the Río Coco in Nicaragua; Juan Felipe Herrera in Califas; and Dr. José Cuellar, a.k.a. Dr. Loco of the Rocking Jalapeño Band, who provided much need gasolina. José David Saldívar, Emilio Bejel, and Pablo Armando Fernández, for their support in Havana, Cuba, via Casa de las Americas. Thank you my brothers. Kim Addonizio who suggested a title. The younger set, my students, who often taught me. Mi jefe—el mero, mero. El Santo Señor de Chalma. My familia (I see Marisol admiring the ocean). And all my relations, muy agradecido. Abrazos y besos.

For Magaly Fernández
who is called Love

# CONTENTS

# Boy on a Wooden Horse

The end of August, 1956. A Saturday in Mexico City. In my black charro outfit bought especially for today's occasion, I go with La Guela to Mercado La Merced. La Guela is my tight-fisted grandmother under whose care I live. She grips my wrist with her claw of a hand and hauls me aboard the bus. "Sombras," by Javier Solís, the newest idol of the Mexican public, is blaring from the radio. We squeeze through the bus till a man with a hat gives us his seat, and I climb on La Guela's bony lap. She is taking me to have my photograph taken. With a puff on his cigarette, the driver forces the stick shift into gear and the bus lurches forward. He wipes the back of his neck with an oily handkerchief and looks at me through the oblong mirror that has a decal of a naked woman. A plastic Virgen de Guadalupe is glued to the dashboard. The red fringe across the windshield bobs up and down as the bus chugs through traffic, thick with cars and noisy claxons. The driver's cigarette and the diesel fumes make me dizzy, but I fight off the nausea by thinking of Mother.

I am Mundo, a six-year-old fierce capricho of a boy, a walking tantrum and a torment for La Guela. She threatens me when I don't behave, like this morning, when I rolled one calcetín over the other. She cried in frustration when she couldn't find the sock that was there all along. Then on our way out the door she pointed a crooked finger in my face, "After the mercado, watch out those robachicos don't snatch you." Her words shrivel me up. This morning La Guela said I could easily be lost in this city of a million strangers. The streets are dangerous, teeming with robachicos, boogiemen who snatch children from buses then dig out their eyes, cut off their tongues, and force them to beg in the streets.

Every afternoon La Guela burns scented candles that make me cough while she kneels in the living room before chrome photos of her saints. She is so sinister in her holiness the cackle of her prayers scares me. Sometimes my sister Meche and I have to kneel on the tile floor and pray with her. La Guela says the Devil is the Prince of Darkness and our sins are to blame for everything. At night, my personal demons gather behind closet doors; brujas hide in every darkened corner; Satan himself lurks in the bathroom, ready to pounce on little boys. La Guela, this brittle woman dressed in black, with an eye cloudy as an oyster, an eye that looks at me without seeing, controls me with the power of fear.

On the bus, stiff on La Guela's lap, I close my eyes and pretend I am blind, that my hands are cut off, that I'm missing a leg. I imagine a world without light, a world without my sister's radiant eyes, a world without Mother, her beautiful face that gives meaning to life. I much prefer my sight. I am the pampered son of a future star of Mexican cinema whose glossy studio portraits adorn our house. I don't believe in saints; it's to Mother's photo I pray at night before falling asleep.

As we near the mercado the cries of street vendors offering tomatoes and chilis compete with the shouts of boys running alongside the bus selling newspapers— "¡Excélsior! ¡El Excélsior!" The monotonous windows of gray apartment houses, replicated a hundred times, reflect the cloudless sky. We pass a building under construction made entirely of glass and chrome. This is La Capital before the earthquake of 1957, before sanctioned greed picks clean the bones of its citizens, before pollution smothers the Ahuehuete trees in Chapultepec Park, turning them yellow as old tobacco. But on this Saturday, at least for the moment, Mexico City is a magnificent metropolis, the grandest city in the world, the Paris of the '20s, the Madrid of the '30s, the New York of the '40s, all blended together in its cafés and cinemas. It boasts of famous muralists, exotic painters, sensuous poets, legendary screen actors, and the most beautiful dusky women of this century, Dolores del Río, María Félix, Toña La Negra, the poetess Pita Amor, and the fashion model María Asúnsulo, mujeres muy hembras, capricious and arrogant. And also on this list because she is beautiful and berrinchuda—Mother, her light still reaching me, still illuminating the dark roads I travel.

La Guela and I have come across town to La Merced from Calle Niño Perdido. We share a crumbling colonial house with two other families, the Navarros and the Sendenios, and the paper-thin walls cannot hide the disaster of our lives. My parents are divorced, a major scandal in the Mexico of that era. Mother, strong-willed and intelligent, as well as beautiful, comes from New Mexico, the little town of Belén. Her mother—La Guela—lives in mourning, honoring her dead. La Guela birthed three sons, none of whom lived to see twenty. Her favorite and youngest, Severio, was killed in the early days of the war in the Pacific, in Corregidor in 1942. After this last tragedy La Guela flees, with her candles and her prayers, to Mexico City and to other sorrows.

As we reach our stop across from Mercado La Merced, the radio announcer breaks into the music with the news of another horrific accident. A bus has plunged off a curve, dragging a dozen citizens to their doom. The driver digs a brown scapular from under his shirt and kisses it. Last night a comet streaked over the city illuminating the sky with a bright orange tail that dripped fire. Panic-driven crowds rushed to the Basilica and prayed till dawn. Meche says it means the end of the world. And Meche never lies.

◆

All my childhood memories unwind in black-and-white, as if my life was either light or shadows, without a middle ground. I recall those years like a series of cinematic dissolves and fade-outs, scenes that blend into each other, a montage of close-ups and quick cuts—Mother's perfect face as she lines her mouth with lipstick; Meche, with her big eyes, pretty as a hibiscus, singing rancheras; La Guela's wrinkled face, praying to her saints. I remember Mexico City as if I'm seeing it through an overhead shot from a helicopter: Avenida Reforma is a wide-angle shot, straight and lined with glass and chrome high-rises, the ancient trees arching over the dense traffic. The elegant avenue is intersected with glorietas and statues mounted on pedestals, heroic Cuauhtémoc, Columbus, El Caballito. My favorite is the golden Angel with outstretched wings at the entrance to Chapultepec Park, the glorious symbol of the city. To me, the Angel is the naive hope of my youth, the future we all dreamed would come with golden wings and lead us to paradise. The Mexico City of my childhood is a city of illusions, a city of dreams, where the lotería nacional turns homeless paupers into millionaires overnight. It is a glamorous city, and it fits Mother like a hundred-peso hat. She loves to relax in the mornings in her red robe, sipping her coffee, enjoying the view from our patio of Popo and Ixta, those eternal lovers, stunningly visible on the horizon. For lunch she likes Sanborn's, where she runs into movie stars like Arturo de Cordova and María Félix.

My father is an accountant for Pemex, a step up from his previous job in a shoe factory. He puts in thirteen- and fourteen-hour days trying to keep the books straight, but there's so much graft he is driven to despair. I often overhear him complain to Mother—How am I supposed to balance the Chief's accounts when he doesn't know how much he's stolen this month? Mother shrugs. She is preparing to abandon ship and the fortunes of Petroleos Mexicanos, the national oil company, mean nothing to her.

My sister Mercedes—all I ever call her is Meche—has big luminous eyes, eyes that see farther than other people, that look great on a virgin saint or a martyr. What is my first memory of Meche? She is in a park—La Alameda? Pedestrians are handing her coins because they think she is performing for her supper, but Meche is singing rancheras because she likes to shout, pegar gritos with all her heart. The Catholic school nuns say that Meche is a genius, that she has a remarkable memory able to recall after one reading the entire contents of Hardy's *Life of the Saints*. But Meche doesn't love saints, she loves Chabela Vargas, Lucha Reyes, and Lola Beltrán, and she knows all their sad songs. My parents call her La Divina, a divine angel. Every morning, La Guela plaits Meche's hair in a tight black braid that swings behind her like a rope tying her down to the Mexican earth.

Mother, movies, songs, all jumbled together, create my childhood memories. Meche and I are in the Cine Colonial; the audience is hushed while up on the big screen Pedro Infante sings "Mi nana Pancha." The movie is *Escuela de Vagabundos*, and behind Pedro Infante we can see Mother, who is wearing braids—which she never does at home—and a white blouse that makes her look poor, because she is an extra in this scene and Pedro Infante is playing a jobless vagabond. A beam of pure light projects Mother's face on the screen and the theater grows hushed before her radiant features. When the camera pans in for a close-up of Mother, my eyes fill with tears of joy. It is this image of Mother that is a freeze-frame in my memory. I stare lovingly at her beautiful face, the penciled brows, her fabulous eyes. Mother's face, the size of a movie screen, fades in and out of all my childhood memories, but the edges are always blurred, the image never clearly focused. When I picture Mother, I think of her as pure light, puritita luz. Meche is an angel, the lunar light that peers in through the Venetian blinds, playing on my face when I'm trying to sleep. Sometimes I think those years in Mexico City are really a movie I saw at the Cine Alamo or at the Cine Colonial. I'm confused by the illusion, but accept it as reality.

La Guela and I are going across town that Saturday to take my picture so it can be sent to Mother, who is spending a month in Acapulco. She has gone to the famous resort to film commercials, some of the first for Mexican television. I have seen her appear on the neighbor's TV set. She was holding a bottle of aspirin and saying something like "Nada mas que Cafiaspirina me quita el dolor de cabeza." Then she smiled. Meche and I are ecstatic when we see Mother on television but La Guela purses her lips and says nothing. Mother is an aspiring actress who has appeared in several productions as an extra, *Llevame en Tus Brazos*, with Ninón Sevilla, and the forgettable *Secretaria Peligrosa*, in which she actually has two lines: "Aquí esta su café. ¿No gusta algo mas?"

But she is being groomed to be a future star, already being touted as the next Dolores del Río. Mother is a stunning beauty, her hair smooth as obsidian, her eyes dark pools, big enough for every Mexican male to swim in. These commercials she is filming in Acapulco will open the doors to fame and riches for her, or so she hopes, or so we all hope.

◆

At La Merced, the photographer places the wide sombrero at a rakish angle, revealing my smooth forehead. He fixes the lights on my round face and I stare at the camera with the sharp intensity of a six-year-old, dressed in his first charro outfit decorated with twisty white braids around the collar and along the arms and down the pant seams. I am mounted on a wooden horse painted with dots to resemble a pinto, but with no pretense at reality since in the photo can be seen quite clearly that the horse is mounted on a stand.

My left hand holds the horse's reins in the proper underhand manner, my right hand grips the handle of a big pistol buckled around the waist, a lariat hangs from the pommel. The edge of the backdrop is decorated with painted geraniums, maguey plants, and organ cactus, and in the center there's the two volcanoes, Popo and Ixta. A flock of swallows flies through the painted sky, above them white chubby clouds and a propeller plane with the markings of the Mexican flag.

An instant before the photographer snaps the picture and the flash fixes me forever on the wooden horse, my right shoelace unravels like a string on a top.

◆

Mother celebrated her quinceañera in Mexico City with a white dress from El Palacio de Hierro. At the end of World War II she is a nineteen-year-old stenographer in the Department of Public Works. She goes to the movies every Saturday with her friends; they have coffee afterwards on Insurgentes, or go window shopping in La Zona Rosa. Then she meets my father, a galán in a pin-stripe suit with orchids on his tie.

They honeymoon in Vera Cruz and Meche is born the following year. Four years later, while they're on vacation in Hollywood, my father breaks his left leg in a car accident. Mother is eight months pregnant. They decide to stay till my father recuperates. That's why I am born in Hollywood, USA, in a small stucco hotel on Cahuenga Boulevard, a stone's throw from the Hollywood Walk of Fame. I will be the second and last child of this marriage, a native son of California but raised in Mexico, La Capital.

On their return to Mexico City, my father pays someone off and gets hired by Pemex, and their lives settle into the rich monotony of work and occasional nights out, until the afternoon a producer sees Mother having lunch at Sanborn's, in La Casa de Las Azulejas. He is Fernando de Fuentes, chief of production for Diana Films, and he offers Mother a role in a movie; the movie is *Escuela de Vagabundos*, the leading actor is the biggest star in Mexican cinema, Pedro Infante. Her first role lasts barely three minutes, but she is swept up in the glamour and make-believe of the movies. An avalanche of parties and gala dinners follows. My father feels uncomfortable around these Churubusco studio big shots, but he escorts her anyway. They attend the film opening at the Teatro Chapultepec. Later, when Mother talks about that magical evening, she will recall the fountain in the lobby bubbled pink champagne instead of water. I hear these stories from my father when I'm older, but I am too young to remember exactly when the movie premiered.

Her debut in *Escuela de Vagabundos* is followed by minor roles, promises and offers of bigger roles the following year. Fernando de Fuentes is having a script written for her and Mother decides to pursue a movie career, which leads to the big break up. My father admires everything from the Unites States; Mother strives to be more Mexican than the Mexicans. My father wants a typical middle-class life, but Mother wants everything, and she wants it now. These are the irreconcilable differences that rend them asunder.

When Mother announces her intention to change her name to Amelia Zea, our apartment on Calle Bucareli is the setting for angry scenes. I recall loud music on the radio, followed by lots of arguing and shouting while my father drinks one 'jaibol' after the other.

"You're a married woman with two kids. Forget that tontería."

"I want my own life, something more than this."

"This isn't good enough for you? Have it your way. But I won't stick around."

"No one's asking you to."

Then my father packs a suitcase and leaves. For a while, Meche and I have ugly sibling fights because she supports our father, and I—I am in love with Mother. She is a goddess who can do no wrong, and I worship at her altar.

Soon we cannot afford the apartment on Calle Bucareli so we move to Niño Perdido where the rents are cheaper. This is the decaying house Meche calls "the swamp." The tiles are worn to the dirt, mold breeds in every crack, and paint curls away from the walls. La Guela complains about our neighbors she refers to as those "pelados." But through all this Mother dresses elegantly, wears white gloves and little hats with black veils like a model that just stepped out of a photograph.

We have no phone so Mother takes her calls at the corner pharmacy, and Dr. Martínez sends a boy to tell her when she's wanted. She is struggling to find work as an actress and seems to be always waiting for an important call. In the meantime she paints her nails, applying each stroke of the tiny brush with the precision of a surgeon. Or she sits before her vanity, trying on make-up, and lets me watch. I love it when she brings out her make-up, her nail polish, her blush, the mascara, the combs, the cut-glass atomizer, and goes through the ritual painting, spraying, and trying on different looks, different hair styles, five different shades of lipstick. It's like a game for me, watching her become all the different women she is. "What do you think of this color, amorcito? Do you think it makes me look too dark?"

I think she looks beautiful in every shade of red. She keeps the radio tuned to XEW and she adores the songs of María Luisa Landín, especially "Amor Perdido," which is all the current rage. At the end of this ritual that lasts for hours, Mother is gloriously transformed into Amelia Zea, future star of movies and television. Some days I haven't eaten a bite, but what do I care? Hunger only sharpens my senses to her beauty.

♦

La Capital is a city of extremes. On Avenida de la Reforma I admire long sleek automobiles driven by chauffeurs in uniform. Through television and the movies I glimpse the lazy luxury of the rich. But I am overcome by a strange sadness the first time I see a trajinero, one of those desperate men who strap chairs to their backs and carry old people or invalids for a peso. We are saved from the stench of the open sewers outside the zaguán by the almond trees that bloom in the courtyard, drifting their fragrance into our house.

My refuge is the gnarled almond tree outside our door, where propped on its branches I snap pebbles at birds with my slingshot. My other toy is a yellow top with red stripes. I can make the top dance between my fingers, into my palm, where it spins happily; the lead point doesn't hurt but tickles like one of Meche's kisses.

On Fridays the man who sharpens knives comes around blowing a reed flute; the vegetable seller turns the corner in his red and yellow wagon; the camote seller hisses his presence with a steam whistle and a raspy voice that shouts, "¡C-a-a-a-a-m-o-o-tes! Tres por un peso!" The candy man Cayetano sets up his wooden box of amber cone pirules and golosinas outside the iron-grilled door. The palomilla of chavalos who play in the courtyard is made up of Ñengo, whose eyes drip yellow tears, and his brother Chucho, who stutters. My best friend is La Liebre, who owns a thousand freckles, he is my mero nero. He is eight and doesn't know how to read, but he can count to a hundred.

Ñengo is our leader, stocky and tough as a pit bull. He brings us *Vodevil*, the macho magazine with drawings by Vargas and sepia photos of Tongolele, the striptease dancer, in garters and high heels. He's also good at stealing a handful of sweets as he runs by Cayetano, slivers of candied papaya, or squares of red and white coconut he shares with us behind the lavanderias where the women wash clothes. Cayetano's beard is linty and stained with coffee. His coat is covered with different colored patches. Sometimes he gives La Liebre and me a free candy, but then he tries to pinch our crotch, and says he wants *our* pírul. So we make fun of him and his straw hat.

One day La Liebre takes me to his house in another colonia. We walk for blocks then ride a bus then walk some more. The city is so huge that we wander the labyrinth streets by instinct and sense of touch. He leads me to an alley, smelly with urine. In the dark flooded passageway I hear rats grinding their teeth as they scurry around our shoes. La Liebre lives behind a yellow door, in an unlit, ominous hovel. The walls are made of cardboard nailed over wooden frames. He sleeps behind a dirty blanket hung on a string; his bed is a petate, a straw mat he shares with two brothers and a sister. The place feels abandoned, like no one has lived here in a hundred years. La Liebre discovers a cigarette butt in a pile of trash and we sit on the dirt floor while he takes a few puffs. He tells me about sex but I don't believe him. So he drops his pants and shows me his paloma, then makes it grow with his hand. It's something I know nothing about. He laughs. "You'll see your father screwing your mother one day," he says.

The words are barely out of his mouth when I shove him to the ground. He tries to get up but I shove him down again. I stand over him angry as a fire ant. "Take it back buey." He smiles with rotten teeth, his pinga still hanging out of his pants. "Don't be a cabrón," he says, and offers me the butt. I try his smoke. *¡Tos! ¡Tos!* My head spins like the silver-winged horse in the merry-go-round of Chapultepec Park and Mother's face appears surrounded by kleig lights. I refuse to think of Mother as anything but a pure and perfect angel.

◆

I much prefer the streets where I am free of La Guela's tyranny. Somehow my cuates, Ñengo, Chucho, La Liebre, and I escape drowning in the nearby river when we go swimming; somehow, we are not crushed by buses or the religious fears propping up heaven. At night, la palomilla comes to our apartment, and Meche adjusts the bakelite knobs of our Phillips radio to "Cuentos de Misterio," and we stretch out on the floor, losing ourselves in the stories of Edgar Allan Poe, or we share the latest Jorge G. Cruz photonovelas of El Santo, the masked wrestler who is our idol. Of this palomilla I have forgotten their real names if I ever knew them. We will mature like in speeded-up film, we will become young men within the coming year. These memories blend into each other without set frames; in one I'm a six-year-old boy listening to the radio, the next minute I'm that same boy in an abandoned shack smoking cigarettes. The approaching months will tear our childhood from us, will maim and deform us, will leave us dazed and stunned.

◆

As Mother becomes ever more busy with her career, La Guela takes over the task of raising me. She demands devotion to her saints, but her endless praying bores me. When I'm forced to kneel with her, I mix up the prayers so she becomes confused—Our Mother who art in heaven . . . . I don't need to cross the ocean to see fanatics. Every Sunday morning La Guela wraps a black rebozo over her head and follows the crowds to the Tepeyac where devotees of La Virgen de Guadalupe cross the stone plaza on their knees, leaving bloody trails on the lava bricks. I see women faint before the Virgen's candle-lit altar, grown men wipe tears from their mustaches. On Ash Wednesday I make a giant scene when the priest tries to mark my forehead with ashes. I scream and squirm till La Guela drags me out of church, angry as the devil, but I wipe the ash cross off my forehead, anyway.

La Guela says I am born in Los Unai. I am from the other side. "You're a Pocho," she says. "You aren't Mexican at all." I want to know what she means. But she loses herself in mumbled prayers and I forget what she has said. By now I believe she is completely crazy.

In counterpoint to La Guela, Mother allows me everything, even keeps me home from school. I'm a precocious boy, teaching myself to read at the age of four. Mother thinks this is charming and has me read to her friends, budding starlets who smile when I read aloud the society pages of *El Excélsior*. These young actresses are impeccably dressed, stylish women, their heads filled with stars, their bosoms with perfume, they plant kisses on my forehead that leave me spinning.

◆

I am first conscious of desire one afternoon when Mother returns from the salon in Polanco where she has her hair done. She is stunningly beautiful that day, all manicured and perfumed, her hair in short curls; I am in awe of her. She stands at our door and says to me, "I told my hairdresser I couldn't pay him till next week. And you know what he said amorcito? 'Never mind. It's my pleasure.'"

Even then I know she has irresistible charm, a face to launch her to fame and stardom. She removes her high heels and curls up on the chenille bedspread for a nap. She is wearing a dark silk dress that clings to her hips, revealing her shapely legs the color of cognac. I watch her sleeping. I'm fascinated by the curve of her hips, the sheen of her nylons, her breasts rising and falling, her face in repose. A powerful and painful emotion strikes me: I am in love with Mother, and I will kill any man who hurts her. I'm sure of this—I want this slumbering angel to myself. At the same time I'm confused by my desire, I don't know what it means. I don't have the words to explain what I feel. How can I be worthy of an angel?

✦

Months after we have moved to Calle Niño Perdido, my father appears one night and takes me to a boxing match at La Plaza de Toros. Eighty thousand screaming Mexicans are rooting for Ratón Macias. The cigar smoke and the heat make me nauseated. My father has to carry me outside, where he listens to the fight on the loud speakers. Then we go to Insurgentes and in the middle of the celebrating mobs, my father jumps on a car hood and, waving his hat, he shouts till he's hoarse, "¡Viva México! ¡Viva México!" It's the one and only time he is proud of being Mexican. Another time he takes Meche to the circus in Puebla and I have a tantrum only Mother can comfort. She holds me in her arms after my father leaves, and coddles me—her precioso. My face is covered with tears and her perfume, and I want to be forever sheltered in her arms.

Later that night, she has me help her get dressed. She keeps her silky underthings in drawers scented with dried gardenias. I unfold the nylon stockings she will roll over her beautiful legs, and I see how she snaps them in place with garters. I am the one who stands on a chair and zips her up. "Amorcito, you understand I have to go out don't you? I need to meet those big-shot producers. That's the only way a girl will get those good roles. And those are the only ones that count, precioso." Then she leaves with her actress friends and I'm alone with La Guela.

Once Mother goes out for the night, La Guela starts in. Her voice, shrill and bitter, hints of scandal and the fires of damnation. "What is this world coming to? Who can believe the way those women dress, if I didn't know better I'd say they were rameras, prostitutes. God will punish them because He sees everything we do."

I don't listen to La Guela; instead I stare at Mother's studio portrait on the wall, more beatific than Father Pio's. I fall asleep past midnight, curled asleep on the floor, waiting for Mother to come home. Mother doesn't appear till the next morning, by then La Guela's rage has simmered down to a smouldering ember. But I am so grateful when Mother returns that I rush to hug her and smother her face and hands with kisses.

Then a tall, handsome man with a mustache appears to comfort Mother. They spend many afternoons riding around the city in his white Chrysler convertible that is the talk of the colonia. She tells me they are just friends. "He's married," she confides, "but that doesn't make him a devil, does it amorcito?"

Mother has two great loves, the movies—and window-shopping. She spends hours in front of display windows admiring furniture; sometimes I think the nickel-plated living room set in the front window of Salinas y Rocha is ours. After one of these all day excursions with Mother and La Guela, we wind up in the palm-filled lobby of the Hotel Reforma, where the man with the mustache is waiting. I am not allowed in the heavily chromed Chrysler. Mother drives off with the handsome man leaving me with La Guela.

♦

The photo of me on the wooden horse will be mailed to Mother in Acapulco. She will carry the photo in her suitcase along with her perfume—Schiaparelli's "Shocking" is her favorite—her silk stockings, her make-up, her beautiful dresses, a book of poems by Pita Amor, the script that has been written for her, "Las Mil Y Una Noches," a role that will later go to María Antonieta Pons, and a scarf in which she has wrapped a dried gardenia. Her boyfriend at the time—she has dumped the idol and is now seeing Alvaro Baena, a cinematographer—will pack her suitcase in the trunk of the pearl white 1954 MG convertible they will drive back to Mexico City. She will be madly in love with Alvaro when they leave Acapulco. It will be the last day she will be in love.

Amelia Zea, destined to be a star of Mexican cinema, will drive the sports car for the first hour; when the hairpin curves of the highway make her dizzy, they stop in front of a roadside restaurant. Alvaro buys her a 7-Up and takes over the driving. She will be sitting in the passenger seat, trailing a ribbon of smoke from a Casinos cigarette, her favorite brand. She'll have her long hair tied back with a silk scarf, a gift from an admirer. Her head will be filled with memories of Acapulco, the Hotel Guacamaya, drinking highballs at poolside, and whatever other fun she might have experienced with Alvaro. Perhaps her thoughts will touch on my father, or on one of her other lovers, perhaps they will touch on Meche or even on me.

When she gets tired she rests her head on Alvaro's shoulder as he drives, so she will not see the truck that passes them on the left, that cuts too sharply in front of them and shakes her awake with the frightening sound of brakes screeching. The sudden bone-crushing force throws her forward into the windshield as the sports car collides with the cement-loaded truck and Alvaro is hurled from the vehicle to an instant and merciful death, while Mother is left broken in the crumpled interior of the MG.

When my father is notified of the accident, nearly twelve hours later, he rushes from his office in the Pemex building and hurries to her bedside in the hospital at Taxco. She has suffered multiple injuries, internal hemorrhaging, cuts and abrasions on her face, but worst is the broken vertebra that leaves her paralyzed. She cannot move from the neck down, only her eyes hold any spark of life.

My father arranges for an ambulance to take her to the Hospital Inglés in Mexico City, and he rides with her, keeping watch over her now fragile beauty. Before he leaves Taxco, he goes to the site of the accident.

The MG is a twisted mess of steel pushed to the side of the road; the suitcases, her clothes and jewelery are all gone. He gathers from the roadside whatever belongings have not been scavenged and brings back pages of the script, the book of poems with the cover smudged with grease and dirt, and the photo of me on the wooden horse, crimped at one corner, as if someone had considered, then decided against taking it.

The next two days Mother goes in and out of conscious-ness, in and out of deliriums in which she hallucinates herself as a young girl in the fields of Belén playing with her brothers. My father takes a twenty-four hour vigil at her bedside, sleeping on a cot, calling all over the country till he finally locates a specialist in Guadalajara, who agrees to come see her. Meche and I visit on the second day, and Mother does not recognize us. Her face is purple with bruises; only her eyes, those dark stars, reveal the woman she is. I kiss her bruised forehead. When I leave my vision is blurry. I will never see her again. Before the spe-cialist can arrive, she dies at three in the morning, my fa-ther at her side.

It rains on the day of Mother's funeral. Before we leave for the crematorium, Meche takes scissors to her braid and snip, snip, separates herself from her childhood. Amelia Zea's friends, the hopeful starlets all show up. Fernando de Fuentes, who discovered Mother in Sanborn's, says a few words. Delia Magaña, the first of their group to make it big, hires a ten-piece orchestra to play in the lobby of the cre-matorium, "Amor Perdido." There is no priest, no prayers, no absolution. Her ashes are sent to my father, La Guela will not have them.

Afterwards, they all come to our house and the grim Guela serves coffee. Mother's friends tell stories about her, they nibble on pan dulce, wipe the powdered sugar from their lips, and cry big trembling sobs into their scented hankies. They bid farewell to Amelia Zea in the name of the close-up, the wide-angle shot, and the Cinemascope.

◆

After Mother's funeral the house in Niño Perdido turns into a bedlam of prayers and evil brujas that curse my life with La Guela. Darkness terrifies me. At night La Llorona hides in closets and I dream of buildings burning, with charred skulls and hands raining down on me. I spend most of my days with La Liebre. If before, La Guela instilled in me fear for the smoke-belching buses, now I ride the back bumpers, hopping on as they stop for lights on Pino Suarez. I turn insolent with La Guela; I curse her and stay out late, often coming home at midnight, sometimes later. I become a six-year-old impossible to control, angry at the world.

La Liebre is a street-wise kid, he hangs with the teporochos, steals from the mercaderas, and shows me how to smoke grifa. We twist the brown grifa into pitos with strips of *El Excélsior* and sneak into the Teatro Alamo to see movies of Tin Tan, or Resortes. From the mambo-dancing, caló-rapping zoot-suiter Tin Tan, I learn my first words of English—"oqaí," "guan momen," "whassamarer," "shaddup." When we don't have grifa we smoke cigarette butts scavenged from the gutters. Or I steal copper coins from blind newsellers, or La Liebre steals pesos from the candy man, and we drift off, smoking grifa and sipping coffee around trash-can fires, laughing at the billboard neon fireworks that light up the Mexico City nights. This is my age of childhood in a city that no longer exists. This is the world I travel sightless, aimless as a beggar, without hope or redemption, chingas o te chíngan.

Then La Liebre disappears without a trace, vanishes into the maze of the city, with Cayetano the candy man. I'm left to wander the streets alone. I come home only when I'm exhausted. If Meche is feeling better, there's merienda waiting for me, a snack of hot chocolate and pan dulce. Sometimes only a glass of milk. Sometimes nothing. La Guela no longer calls me Mundo, but my full name, Reymundo, as if I'm now grown up and must leave behind my childhood name.

Months go by. I'm now seven. I'm in Plaza Garibaldi waiting for a drunk to fall asleep on a bench so I can go through his pockets when a voice calls me over.

—Órale cuatacho.

I barely recognize La Liebre. He's covered with dirt from sleeping on the streets, or in worse places. He says he couldn't take it with the candy man anymore. I don't ask what it is he couldn't take—but La Liebre tells me what Cayetano did, and I cannot look my best friend in the eye. When he's finished, it's like he's someone I don't know anymore. We're like two kids on a sinking boat doomed to watch each other drown. So we hatch a plan to run away, maybe to Vera Cruz, or Merida, anywhere to get away from this nightmare.

I tell him, "Meet at my house in the morning, early, I'll take some pesos from La Guela, y nos largamos a la chíngada."

I cannot sleep all night. As soon as my lids close, devils appear with eyes like candles. Way before daybreak I crawl out of bed and sneak into La Guela's room. The creaking floorboards sound loud as thunder. She keeps her money in a coffee can hidden behind a statue of La Virgen. I reach in without disturbing her and withdraw a fistful of pesos. Then I look one last time at Meche, who is sleeping off some medication, and place a tender kiss on her forehead. The courtyard is empty, icy. A rooster-colored moon hangs over me as I make my way through the shadows to the zaguán where La Libre is waiting for me. The silence is so heavy the city appears dead.

I cross the courtyard but I stall at the entrance of the zaguán. Something holds me back. I call for La Liebre, call again. I see someone or something moving in the shadows. Then out of the darkness Cayetano's bearded face appears. I suffocate when he puts his arm around my shoulder. His hand tightens around my neck, "I've been waiting for you," he says. His fingers smell of ether. I can't breathe; all I can do is whisper, "Don't hurt me." I can't tell if this is a dream, but just in case, I suddenly wail like a siren. At that same instant the earth starts trembling, the walls sway, a rumble rises from the bowels of the earth that rattles every bone in me. As I break free of Cayetano's grip and leap back into the courtyard, the zaguán crumbles with a terrific roar and an explosion of dust. I see our house swaying, then the apartment building next door collapses like a house of cards, and a powerful blast shakes the courtyard with such force that it knocks me down. A hundred screams splinter the night. I hear babies wailing. More screams, countless sirens, the world is coming to an end.

I wake up in the courtyard with La Guela and Meche hugging me, their faces wet with tears of terror. It's the morning of July 28, 1957. Smoke blots out the pale morning sun, the survivors gathered in the courtyard are delirious with total panic. Señora Sendenio, still in her robe, is stumbling around all dazed. One wall of our house is missing. Sirens pierce the sky. A powerful earthquake has destroyed the city. The golden Angel on La Reforma has fallen and lies shattered in pieces as if it were not made of bronze but of plaster. "Ay, Dios mío, dios mío, what will we do," La Guela screams. The city is without electricity or water. The ten-foot wall around our house is dust. Where the zaguán once stood there's a pyramid of bricks, rubble, and twisted rebars. Meche says I was sleepwalking; that's why they found me knocked out in the courtyard. La Guela thanks La Virgen for my safety. I don't say a word when the Green Cross medics come by asking about survivors trapped in the ruins.

The weeks that follow are a blur. The skyscrapers on La Reforma are abandoned, skeletal. A four-story retail store has collapsed like a limp balloon. Four blocks away, the ultra-modern pharmaceutical building is a mountain of broken glass. Everywhere the bones of the city are showing like some newly unearthed pre-Columbian ruins. The house where we lived is condemned and we move to my cousin Arturo's house in San Angel. Heavy rains follow the earthquake as if even the Virgen of Guadalupe had abandoned her children. In the outskirts of the city those without homes are drowned or washed away by the rampaging waters. In the Zócalo, furniture, sofas and TVs float out the doors of houses. After the rains, a hurricane wind rips tiles from roofs and knocks down trees in La Alameda. We hear rumors about plagues, thousands dead, whole colonias gone, and entire towns buried in the countryside. Frightened crowds mob the Tepeyac to pray for deliverance. But there is no deliverance, nowhere to hide.

Everyday La Guela tells us our father is going to take us to Los Unai, that he will save us. But at night we huddle in the park of San Angel and sleep beneath ominous stars that seem to mock our fate.

Several months after the earthquake, our plane tickets finally arrive. La Guela, who is coming with us, hires a taxi to the airport—Meche is dressed in white and I'm in a dark suit with tie, and black polished shoes. When we arrive at the airport, a huge four-prop plane modern as the country we are going to is revving its motors on the tarmac. Soon the line of people starts boarding the TWA plane and La Guela grabs Meche by the elbow and I take her hand and together we go up the metal staircase, into the whirlwind of the engines that suck us into another vortex. I am happy, we are leaving the ruins of the city of dreams.

I will not see Mexico City again till I am nineteen. By then the city will be a congested pit of decay and corruption, its wide avenues lined with human debris and portraits of El Presidente on every telephone pole and tree. I return just before the 1968 Olympics, when the army unleashed its fury against the students in Tlatelolco. I saw what was done and the lies to cover it up. But that's not the

Mexico City that I knew, the city of my childhood.

A long time ago I promised myself there was no point in looking back. I never saw La Liebre again or heard whatever became of him. Ñengo and Chucho disappeared into the streets like phantoms. Years later I came across a photo in *Alarma!* of two brothers arrested for car theft, and I thought that it could be them. I have never been back to Niño Perdido. But sometimes I can't help but return to Mexico City in my memory, dig around in those ruins of my childhood for an overlooked scene that will explain who I am. When I sit at my desk and look at the photo of myself as a boy on a wooden horse, it reminds me of where I come from, and that fate unravels faster than a shoelace on a six-year-old's shoe. And with those memories burning vivid as the afternoon sun on the Victorian rooftops, I pick up a pencil and begin to write.

The end of August, 1956. A Saturday in Mexico City.

# El Último Round

La Betsy and I were having a bruising, brawling, bare-knuckled, alley-cat, Friday-night brawl. Words were our weapons and they cut like razors. I loved this woman and didn't see how fighting was going to help that.

It was summer and we were riding along the coast in her convertible, the top down, sipping rum from a hand-size flask and the chingasos just sneaked up on us, but they'd been simmering for weeks, arguments about money, mostly that I didn't have any, though I was planning on getting my piece of the cake soon. But we had plenty to fight about besides money, and before long our words turned bitter and hateful. We reached a moment of silence on the darkened highway, the silence right before the big pedo.

La Betsy drove over the hunk of some long dead dog and that got her all flared up again.

"Mundo—you are a dog." She could barely squeeze the words out. Maybe it was the rum. But it could've been me. I bring out the worst in her. So I kept quiet and just went for the ride.

The night had started out real good, like bad things usually start out. We'd met for Happy Hour at El Río, two drinks for two bucks. They kept pouring the rum-and-tonics and we kept drinking them. With the heat and the rum, the conversation soon took on a life of its own and La Betsy dropped a few snide remarks about how las mujeres were more right on than the men. But I didn't think anything of it. That was an old fight I had no chance of winning.

Anyway, I didn't want any of her fight. I wanted to kiss her eyebrows, call her mi tamalito de maiz. My exact words from the night before when I was blowing bubbles up her belly. So I reached in the glove compartment for the Luis Miguel tape *Romance*, hoping that would loosen her up and she'd let go of this ancient battle that wasn't my fault. But it wasn't to be.

"Don't touch that casette," she said.

"What's the matter?"

"You. You're what's the matter."

"Now what I'd do?"

"Name something."

"Come on, cariño . . ."

"Forget it. Just forget about us."

She arched her arms over the steering wheel and stared down the freeway like an angry truck driver. I could tell we were weaving between lanes but I didn't want to look. So I tipped the flask and drank my portion of it. In one gulp. I offered her the last corner.

She shook her head. "I sure wouldn't want to be stuck with you on a deserted island, that's for sure."

"You exaggerate."

"No. I mean it, with you it's always me, me, me always. Ya la chingas."

I'm not kidding ése, but I'd had it with La Betsy. The world spilled over with so much war, famine, pestilence that I craved love from my querida. But instead, these men-mujer hassles were forcing wedges between us, wedges that would later drive us apart. But that's another story.

La Betsy knew how to vex me. So she kept at it, goading me, probing me for weakness. "Sisters, we stand up for each other. We do. Not like men, men are puros perros."

"Woof-woof," I said, "bow-wow. So what you doing with me?"

"I love men. I really, truly love men."

That was a good one.

I had to admit La Betsy had everything. A red Mustang convertible, tenure at Berkeley, a Guggenhiem, a loft in La Mission, woman had more than her share. (Did I mention that her body is draped over some fine bones and that her breasts ride high and tight, just how I like them?) While I had a hole in my sock, and I'm nothing to look at on the beach, so parity was hard to establish. La Betsy could say the cruelest, meanest things but twenty minutes later she'd forget she'd said them. Then she'd wonder why I'd be hurt and angry. But if I said something, like the time I pointed out a red pimple on her flat ass while we were doing it, she brooded and sulked for days, accused me of not treating her right.

So what had started out as just another Friday night quickly degenerated. We wielded our metaphoric razors to slash our hearts. Later, the lesser of these wounds would heal, but the rest would scar or turn to other pains that would test our love.

There wasn't much I wouldn't do for Elizabeth Balvina

Longoria, La Betsy, my chulona, whom I had met at the San Francisco Carnival Ball during a steamy night of samba and rum that lasted till about eight the next morning, when I fell asleep in her bed with only my socks on. We'd been making it ever since, six months now, a record mundial, and each kiss still felt like a shower of confetti.

But that night her heart held no love and it seemed like all we'd ever done was fight.

We were at the peak of Devil's Slide and into the winding part of Highway 1, with hairpin turns a thousand feet above the crashing ocean, where many lives had spun out on this dangerous road. That's where she snapped her fingers indicating I could exit any time, "If you can't take a liberated Chicana" —Snap! Snap! —"pues, chíngale baby!"

She didn't stop to let me out either. The ragtop was down and the wind whipped her hair out like the Llorona. La Betsy drove with her eyes narrowed against the sharp headlights of the oncoming traffic, her fingers so tight around the steering wheel I worried she'd snap it. And they'd find us like in those *Alarma!* photos, buckets of blood and severed limbs and, hell, that's the last thing I wanted, even though I had nothing to look forward to but hard times since I was broke, flat busted, and quebrado. Financially embarrassed. Living on unemployment and didn't know where I would sleep next Friday when my rent was due. So my situation was extreme, to say the least. And fighting with La Betsy, who loved to be showered with cariño and politically correct trinkets, wasn't helping my sullen mood any.

I do have some things going for me though, that's why I had La Betsy. I can dance the intricate ochos of the tango without tangling my feet, and I make love in a chorro of Spanish, a real torrent of 'corazoncitos,' plus my chilaquíles are famous. And I'm radical, too radical, that's why I'd lost my job at the community center. I was run out by the moderates, those little farts. The letter of dismissal stated that my approach to teaching homeboys was too innovative. Too out there. Too much. Man, oh, man. So I was worried La Betsy would leave me. I wanted to keep her because she was not only the best hueso I'd ever had, but she also wears corsets and garters when she makes love, so you know I craved more of her good stuff. I meant to love her as hard as I could, as long as I could. Both. And at the same time.

The lights of Half Moon Bay burned just up ahead as I finished the flask of rum.

◆

Half Moon Bay is like a bite taken out of the California coast. Hill and pine country. The English pirate Francis Drake landed here to slap new planks on his ship. Before that, Ohlone Indians roamed the hills along with coyotes and grizzly bears. Lots of bears. The town is two stoplights, three old hotels with worn porches, some shops, and several biker bars, all strung along Main Street. The only thing missing is the hoosegow.

We came in through Main Street, La Betsy looking for a place to park, and I felt like we'd gone fifteen rounds and was ready to call it a Mexican standoff. One more drink, I thought, and we'll head back. La Betsy slowed the convertible in front of The Old Mission Hotel, a crumbling adobe building, maybe the oldest in town.

But I had one last jab for her. "So where were the Chicanas, las girlfriends, while the sword was put to thousands of Central American women?" She couldn't handle that one, so I answered my own question: "Too busy hustling grants from Reagan, Bush & Co. to give a goddamn."

She hit the brakes so hard I almost flew through the windshield.

"Hey, take it easy," I said rubbing my neck. Too late I remembered how La Betsy had padded her way to the top.

"Get out," she said.

"You're not serious."

"Get. Out. Sácale."

It's either/or time, I thought. She'd done this before, at a party in East Palo Alto. Angry that a woman flirted with me, she left me to hitch a ride fifty miles. I, in all truth, was innocent. This was closer to home, but still.

"Corazoncita," I said.

"Don't talk to me. Out, cabrón!" She swung her arm and pointed to the road with a perfectly manicured fingernail.

This was a strange, unfriendly town, with not even a hydrant on the corner for a man's necessities. The only light came from the bowels of the hotel. The orange light said BEER. That sounded good to me. So. I figured a handful of beers and I could walk back. No problema. I left her in the car and hitched up my pants.

"Suave pues," I said, "this looks like el último round."

"Get lost," she replied.

I turned my back to her and headed for the bar, cool as Pedro Arméndariz in a Mexican movie. Each step away from her solid, firm. I don't know why that's how love always ends with me, tanto amor, then—un gacho goodbye.

The bar smelled of stale sweat layered over sawdust and spilled beer. *The End of the Trail*, the painting of a beaten-down Indian on a worn-out pony, his lance dragging the ground, hung above the bar mirror. A body slumped over a corner table. A pair of cowboys were watching TV with the sound off—a boxing match, two Chicanos pummeling each other senseless. When the cowboys saw me, they poured salt in their mugs. Now it was dark and quiet. Must be some secret code, I said to myself.

The bartender, a biker type with hairy arms and a black widow tattoo crawling on his neck, greeted me like he'd break my face if I didn't tip him right. So I ordered a Corona and tipped him right. A good rule in weird places.

I chugged down the first beer. I was expecting to hear La Betsy drive off, but I didn't give a cold chíngaso. A man has to keep some pride when he's abandoned. I ordered another beer.

Yes, I was upset. Simón que sí. I worshipped La Betsy. I wanted her to be the last woman I would ever love. If I had to fight with her, I wanted us to be under the bed sheets like two cats yowling; that's why we were lovers. I had all the trouble one man could handle. I was dark, Chicano, and unemployed. And I believed God was female, that she'd hung this big chile relleno on me for a reason, and I had a pretty good idea what that reason was. The way I had it figured, to love females was to love God. And I meant to love them. Till they grew tired of me and moved on. And they usually did.

I leaned into the bar, drinking my beer, thinking La Betsy had moved on. Now I was broke *and* filled with angst and despair over losing her. I didn't know if I could ever find another Chicanita to replace La Betsy. I might have to start checking out the other women in the barrio, like the Nicaragüan women, the Dominican women, the Panameñas, and the Brazileñas, especially the Brazileñas, and all that might take a long time, they were so many. So I had another beer while I figured it out. I was trying to get to that spot where angst and despair vanish, replaced by a feeling of general well being. I intended to keep drinking till I arrived, no matter how long or how many beers it took. Just then the front door flew open and La Betsy stormed in. I didn't have to turn around, I could see her in the bar mirror, coming at me like a nuclear torpedo.

She slammed her keys on the bar and they skidded to a stop right in front of me. I just had to look up. Every one in the bar looked up. Even the guy passed out on the table looked up for a quick second before crashing face down again with a thump. La Betsy's eyes were glowing like hot pennies, and I steeled myself. She had one hand on her hip and a finger in my chest. "How dare you say that about us Chicanas, after all we've done for the movimiento."

Oh, I forgot to mention La Betsy always gets the last word. I couldn't argue with her. When La Betsy gets angry she turns into this beautiful stubborn bitch, just gorgeous with her Zapotec profile like that Indian chief on the buffalo nickel. You see now why I love her?

"Chula, you've come back," I said.

"Answer my question damn it."

I didn't see what difference it would make if I did or I didn't. So I didn't. I looked for the bartender but he was at the far end of the bar shooting liar's dice with the cowboys.

La Betsy came to within an inch of me, her face all distorted with anger. "Answer me or you're one dead Mexican dog," she growled.

Either way I'd lose, so I figured I might as well take that long walk back to the City. I spoke in a low voice, almost a whisper. "I said it 'cause it's true."

She sliced my throat with her eyes.

"Oh, you're a pinche, pinche, oh, I can't find the word for you . . . you . . . ."

What was there to say? My hand accidentally fell on her hip but she slapped it away. My hand that just last night had caressed her entire body, top to bottom. Now I was getting mad, felt like rubbing a grapefruit in her face like Jimmy Cagney in that movie I couldn't remember the name of right that minute. But I said no, no, just love this woman. Ésta mujer.

Then she said, "I want a drink. Get me a drink, cabrón."

Before I could move, she changed her mind. "Forget it,

I'll get it myself. You're useless. Like all men I know."

Her mouth that only yesterday whispered love phrases now stoned me with words. Life was full of mystery. The Mayan calendar, for instance. That was a big mystery to me. And Mayan hieroglyphs, that too. Why didn't my car start this morning? Why do some people in this world drink blood while others eat shit? I didn't have answers to these questions. Like I didn't exactly have the answer to this war between the sexes. In this conflict I was a conscientious objector, a pacifist. I couldn't figure out what panochas and pingas, accidents of birth, had to do with it. And I for sure didn't understand the forces that shoved me into confrontations with my querida. So, some things were turning in my head that maybe La Betsy didn't realize.

I went to the jukebox to break the mood. Nothing but country and rock, only one I recognized, D 7, Los Lobos, "Will the Wolf Survive?" That sounded right. I slipped a quarter in the jukebox and felt a whole lot better with Cesar Rojas wailing some mean left-handed guitar riffs.

I came back to La Betsy and told her how I much I loved her. How I would always love her, to the very end of my life. She said, "Take some poison and prove it." My chulona.

That's when one of the cowboys wobbled over, bow-legged as a bear, his sweat stained hat pulled low over his eyes. He rocked on his heels standing there kinda drunk, and I thought maybe he wanted to say hello. Smoke the peace pipe. Or bum a cigarette.

La Betsy turned her back to him with utter contempt.

The cowboy shifted his eyes and mumbled something

that sounded like, "We fod a long time to git you peeble otta here." Then, without a warning, he threw a punch that clipped my jaw and knocked me back against the bar. I shook the stars out of my head. What da fuck? The pendejo had Sunday punched me. "Oh man," I said to myself, "here we go again." I reached for one of the empty Corona bottles and brought it down over the cowboy's head, smashing through his hat to the skull. BLAM! The long-necked bottle exploded in a hundred shards. I tell you a Corona never felt so good. The cowboy's eyes rolled up as he went down, nose first. His head bounced on the floor making a sound like a melon splitting open. He groaned once and it was good night Miss Ann. He wasn't going to bother us any more.

The other cowboy came at me but without much heart.

"Back off," I said. I could clean his guts out with that broken bottle and he knew it. The bartender reached under the bar and I guessed what he was going for. "You won't need that," I said, knowing I didn't want to go up against whatever he had. La Betsy sat frozen on a barstool, her mouth forming a big cherry O, so I grabbed the keys, took her by the elbow, said, "Let's book," and walked out with her, slowly, not threatening anyone because maybe the bartender had a sawed-off or something like that, but without turning our backs to them, without dropping the broken bottle.

We jumped in her car with me at the wheel. I threw the bottle neck away and fired up the engine, jammed it in reverse, and backed out of there so fast I nearly threw La

Betsy against the dashboard. I peeled rubber down Main Street and when we hit Highway 1 North, we were flying. La Betsy sat back in the seat, shell-shocked, breathing hard like she does in the middle of an intense love mambo.

"You all right mamácita?"

"Ay, ay, I guess . . . ."

"Didn't pee on yourself, did you?"

"You'd like to check, wouldn't you, nasty man."

"I'm your nastiest man," I said.

She threw her arms around my neck. "Ay Mundo, I love you so, hombre mucho malo." She laughed with all her heart in it and I knew things were cool with La Betsy.

I drove the winding highway along the coast, exhilarated, my mouth dry, the top down, the wind blowing in our faces, through our hair, the turbulent surf pounding against the rocky cliffs, and it felt good to be free to run.

On our way back to La Mission we stopped at Rockaway Beach. That's when there were just two hotels, no tourists, and no one to bother you. We were feeling pretty somber after that bad borrachera, so I parked by the breakers, the ocean crashing violently against the shore, the crest of each wave sparkling with silver glitter from some phosphorescent microscopic sea life. We had the top down, and gazed for a while at the sky that went on forever. Stars and galaxies, a zillion of them up there. It's funny we never stop to think about the stars, so far away, maybe already turned to ash for all we know. Then La Betsy and I looked at each other, a woman and a man in a car on planet Earth.

La Betsy scooted next to me, her leg touching mine.

I told her, "Give me a beso."

Her eyes cut me like they had done in the bar.

"Desgraciado," she said, "it's too easy for you." But she said it in a way I'd never heard her say it before, with cariño. And then she fell all over me—kissed my bruised jaw, pressed her lips to my eyes, made me feel good again, and this good feeling made me wonder about us, I mean what we were doing to each other. And about how long we would last. I brushed the hair from her face and just looked at her for a minute, looked at this woman, mi estrella, my star. A meteor cut a long purple streak across the sky. She saw it too. And we kissed again. Slow and sweet. La Betsy and me. How it was suppose to be.

# Rose-Colored Dreams

What is Juanito doing this hour of night, selling roses in the streets of la Mission? Wine-colored, blood-colored, and pink rose buds wrapped in cellophane, stuffed in a plastic bucket half his size. He walks in the restaurant thin as a churro; ten years look like thirty stamped on his forehead. A strong wind could blow him to Daly City or Ocosingo, the mountainous Chiapas town of his birth. All the waitresses and regular customers—the soft-bellied ones and the lean ones, the hard-faced cab drivers, the norteño trios—know Juanito's face, his faded blue sweater, his Mayan profile like a clay pendant from Toniná, his cowlick in black mop of hair.

Juan Cocom Heredia—"Juanito," as his mother calls him—should be home, asleep. You know the place, the apartment building on 17th Street, through the lobby door with busted lock, under the sign that says "No Loitering," past the odor of mildew that curdles your brain, up three floors of rickety stairs with broken handrails, down the hallway where gassed cockroaches lie belly-up below the broken window, sweet home. In bed (actually the mattress on the floor he shares with his older sisters) Juanito will dream of a baseball glove or the perfect tail for a kite, dream a sandia paleta from Latin Freeze on 24th Street, with the one seed always frozen near the bottom.

But the family needs more than dreams. That's why Mamá, two sisters, a baby, Juanito and La Abuela—have traveled by truck and bus, pulled by something stronger than destiny, to this two-room battleground of survival. Right this minute, as Juanito treads Mission Street, Mamá, in the apartment, curls over a pedal-driven Singer sewing machine, zigzagging threads as fine as spider webs, running perfect seams down pants, stitching button holes and collars, late into the pale yellow hours of her seemingly endless nights. The two sisters, Dulce and Primavera, with fingers as delicate as ballerinas', hand-stitch beads tiny as dewdrops on dresses that will retail in Union Street boutiques for hundreds of dollars—of which they will receive twenty-five. The baby will be crying in the cardboard crib, a cough racking his sleep. And La Abuela, lost in dreams thick as cataracts, will be chanting Tzotzil prayers to Mayan gods before an altar of beeswax candles, pink flower petals, and Pepsi Cola bottles. The heavy pom incense unravels in a perfumed string toward the water stain on the ceiling that looks like a map of Latin America.

This isn't Mexico City, where Indian families wrapped in newspapers huddle in icy streets under the Monument to the Revolution; this isn't Tegucigalpa either, where worm-ravaged girls peddle Chiclets on street corners. No. This is California. To be exact, La Mission, San Pancho, Califas, Aztlán, land of palm trees and skyscrapers, where there's dollars enough for cellular phones, sports cars, even mota by the trunkful, where a suitcase of cocaine is as easy to buy as a broken-stemmed rose from Juanito's white bucket.

"Oyé chavalo, how much for that handful of rosebuds?"

Four elf-size fingers go up. Juanito makes change for a twenty as fast as an abacus, returns his tiny fist clenched with crumpled bills. "Gracias," he says, like a man. You tip him a couple of dollars—so what?

Every love-struck couple staring into each other's eyes, every loner occupied with a half-empty beer, even the waitress with tired legs waiting for the end of her shift receives a visit from Juanito. Then, with bucket under his arm, he turns one last time to the faces above the steaming plates before he's out into the neon-lit street, leaving a trail of rose petals dark as sacrificial hearts.

# OFRENDAS

"La vida no vale nada"
—for Oscar García Rubio
en un rincón del cielo Mexicano

The fiesta is rocking by the time I arrive dressed as a campesino calavera, authentic in huaraches and smoking a Delicado. At the door of her storefront loft, La Betsy greets me with a kiss, the white ostrich feather in her floppy hat tickling my nose. She is dressed as a calavera catrina, an elegant lady skeleton, with a green feather boa draped serpent-like around her shoulders and a big purple hat right out of a Diego Rivera mural. La Betsy and I finally gave up loving each other and now we're just friends. We're better friends than we were lovers. This Day of the Dead fiesta is also La Betsy's going away party. Like everyone else I know her rent's been raised and now she is looking to the East Bay. Everything's changing in La Mission, murals destroyed, cheap housing gone, you'd think City Planning was out to kill this barrio.

La Betsy presses a foil-wrapped skeleton candy into my hands and then, with an imperious wave at the fiesta, she says, "Make yourself at home, Mundo. There's enough bones here to make any dog happy."

Some things never change.

Everyone in La Mission is here dressed in some kind of skeleton costume. I can't tell who's who except for the obvious beer belly of Toño's or the unmistakable broad nalgas of an ex-girlfriend. The skeletons could be anyone in the barrio. Dozens of emerald and ruby candles of La Virgen del Tepeyac project shadows of dancing skeletons onto the walls. Clouds of scented copal smoke float toward the twelve-foot ceiling crisscrossed with festive yellow and orange papel picado streamers. That Betsy, she's even slipped a skeleton sweater on her chihuahua, Pete Wilson. Makes the perrito look like a Picasso sculpture.

A zany calavera priest with an orange wig tottering on his head is La Betsy's new boyfriend. I don't know the vato but he's passing around a tray of bite-size candy skulls. Blue squiggles decorate the craniums, baroque loops that spell out names—Beto, Tania, Jorge. I'm sure there's a candy skull with my name on it. I'm here to rumba with La Pelona, bald-headed Ms. Death. I want to blow hot air up her satin dress, kiss her sugary lips, caress the chínga out of her so she'll see I'm not afraid of her embrace. It's the Xicano way of life.

An altar stands in the center of the fiesta, a four-tiered pyramid tall as me, draped with a crocheted white tablecloth. Every level of the altar is covered with ofrendas, offerings to a glorious life and a happy death. On the bottom level a dozen full-sized candy skulls sit between red votive candles and yellow taper candles. The next level has bundles of cempasúchil flowers tied with purple yarn, a cross of woven straw, a punched-tin heart with a dent, a twisty serpent made of red and black beans, a calendar of a big-breasted Aztec princess from Taqueria Pancho Villa, a can of Café Bustelo, and a rubber mermaid. On the next level there's a glow in the dark Virgin of Fatima, ristras of dried red chiles, clay dishes filled with cracked corn, pumpkin seeds, anise seeds, and dried rose petals, a yellow packet of Buena Suerte Powder for Luck Finding Work, an amber Dos XX beer bottle, a pack of Zig-zag papers, an aloe vera plant, a miniature diorama of a calavera family being evicted by a calavera landlord, and some photos in gilt-edged frames. At the top of the altar a stone censer releases gray clouds of copal. The altar, candy skulls, votive candles, and copal incense are humble offerings for a bony, bald-headed vieja stalking La Betsy's Dia de los Muertos fiesta. A hundred years from now, who knows if there'll even be a barrio La Mission, so these artifacts will speak volumes to those who reconstruct the past. But what anthropologists in the future will imagine happened here is anybody's guess.

In the center of the altar hangs a family portrait—the father, mother, three kids, all dressed in church-going clothes—next to a postcard of the Virgin of San Juan de los Lagos spreading the triangle of her cape. The dark faces are lit by the rows of votive candles. They could be that family of migrant workers killed crossing Pacheco Pass last month, their car rammed head-on by an eighteen-wheeler, their tragic lives turned into autumn leaves blowing in the wind. They could be the family that perished in the Gartland Apartments fire on 16th and Valencia, their screams haunting me to this day. I figure there must be a heaven since there's hell enough on earth.

My contribution to La Betsy's altar is a photo of my cousin, Arturo, at the seaside, on the malecón at Vera Cruz. Twenty years ago Arturo posed for a street photographer, and now he appears ghostly in the faded black and white photo with the sunset casting his shadow on the sand. This morning at three a.m. a phone call woke me up. My tía Lucha's voice, scratchy and barely audible, came over the long distance connection from Mexico City. Arturo, my *buti carnal*, is dead of pnuemonia, his lungs collapsed by the lead-heavy air. The news cut me in two, like a clay Aztec statuette, half of me alive and breathing, the other half dead, my rib bones showing. I couldn't go back to sleep so I burned the night away, pacing my room, my head filled with memories. Heaven is an exclusive club; I hope Arturo gets a table in the smoking section so he can enjoy his Delicados. Last year we'd hung out in La Mission at Café Macondo, sucking cigarettes and shots of espresso. His thoughts were clear and his laughter strong. He was writing for *Uno Más Uno*, the Mexico City paper and he hoped to get started soon on the Great Mexican Novel. Now he sleeps with marble angels, his dreams chisled onto a stone tablet.

There was nothing I could do about Arturo's death but honor his life, remember our times together, and soothe the spirits in this world and the next. So as the sun rose bright and cold over the Victorian rooftops I cleaned up an old wooden wine crate and painted it the color of the Mexican sky. Inside the crate I placed a sugar skull, a round black bottle of Gusano Rojo Mezcal from Oaxaca, and some thick brown cigars from Chiapas, thick as pingas. Then I strung a wreath of ajo macho across the top. Above the offerings I pinned a photo of Arturo in the Café Macondo, cigarette smoke swirling over his Indian face. I also set three taper candles on his altar, an album of Roberto Torres y su Charanga Vallenata, and some Delicados, the foil creased just so, with several smokes peeking from the opened pack. Beside the altar I stacked several books, so he could have them in that other barrio, *La Vida Inútil de Pito Perez, Cien Años de Soledad, The Diamond Sutra.* I finished by scattering golden cempasúchil petals over the photo, the books and the altar, on the table where the altar sat, on the floor, into the hallway, out to the street, a trail of golden tears so Arturo could find his way to my place.

Before going to the fiesta I turned myself into a calavera, slapped white make-up on my face, smudged black circles around my eyes, put on my big Michoacán hat, black jeans and a black T-shirt with bones X-rayed on it. Then I took my mournful-self to Harrison and 24th Street, where I drank a bottle of Gusano Rojo Mezcal and waited for the skeleton procession. Soon the sound of drums, claves and tambourines approached up 24th Street, drawing the curious from the bars and restaurants.

The Day of the Dead in La Mission is not exactly a Christian ritual, no reverent high mass, either. Aztec dancers led the procession, swooping and swaying, shuffling and twirling down the middle of 24th Street, pounding leather drums and rattling ankle bells, feathered headdresses bobbing over their braids. A raucous mob of candle-bearing calaveras followed them, lifting their voices in song and laughter, snaking their way through the heart of the barrio like a luminous serpent. Giant matachines, their stilts hidden by baggy pants, danced to a calavera batería playing fast samba riffs on their tambores. Barking dogs trailed the procession, wrought into a frenzy by so many bones. Beautiful brown angel calaveras with wire wings bore candles for the disappeared in Central America, for those snuffed by gang violence in the barrios, for those ravaged by AIDS, for those murdered by racism, for those strangled by evictions, for the dying planet even, and for all those who don't know how to love, the living dead—the truly forever dead. Other calaveras scratched güiros, or rattled seed-filled gourds. Some played reed flutes, clay ocarinas, or shook maracas, making this procession a pagan celebration, everyone powered by laughter and music.

I joined the procession, rapping a beat on the mescal bottle and dancing an Aztec two-step over crushed Styrofoam cups, burned-out candles, and dog turds. The procession snaked down 24th Street, up Balmy Alley, and around Garfield Park. And I longed for the darkest woman to dance a manic merengue with, a bone rattling dance of knees and elbows, a dance to mock La Pelona I could feel breathing dust on my face.

Returning to 24th, the procession detoured around a cat flattened in the asphalt by a truck. Only some ruined fur and a smudge of blood remained. I placed a candle at each broken paw, like an offering, and then a chola placed some more candles at the head and the crumpled tail. Her cholo boyfriend threw in some bottle caps. Another calavera came along and left a wreath of plastic roses. Soon it was a regular holy site, the dead cat remembered with Styrofoam cups, candles, cigarette butts; and plastic flowers—an improvised altar to road kills.

Just as the procession was breaking up, a naughty calavera nurse on roller blades damn near ran me over. Under her half-unbuttoned uniform, a bulging white lace bra revealed breasts that could've revived a dead man. Placing her stethoscope over my heart, she solemnly pronounced, "You look way too alive, you need the kiss of death." She quickly withdrew from her Gladstone bag a giant hypodermic that had written in red felt marker— "Apathy." ¡Qué patín! Then she jabbed the toy needle in my ribs and tipped her head back in a grotesque laugh, "Já, já, já." Before I could grab her, she skated off, gooseing bystanders and distributing general havoc.

†

Tonight I want to feel everything, love everyone, even if it kills me. Men are so afraid these days, we don't know how to love anymore. We're so lost, so out of touch with ourselves, afraid to touch, period. I should know, I'm a love consultant for men, a talk-show host on Radio Libre, a pirate radio station in La Mission. I'm sure you've seen the hand-drawn leaflets of a flaming heart over a skull and crossbones. Every Friday night I host "Doctor Corazón's Clínica de Amor." I give tips on what lingerie to buy that special brown girl for Valentine's Day or New Year's. The right wording to her lawyer when you fall six payments behind on child support. Truffles or roses for her birthday? Come to me, I have the answers. And you should hear the sad calls that come in when I'm on the air. I quote: "I've been making it with this ruka for three months, and still haven't brought her to orgasm. What can I do?" "My huiza is frigid—I can't turn her on even with a blow torch. . . ." I say talk sexy *carnal*, whisper sweet words in her ear, the most erotic of all foreplay. And this poor lost soul who called in the other night—"Doctor, I'm thinking of going to the Penis Institute for an implant . . . ." I railed at him, "Save your cash, homey, the brain's the biggest sex organ we have." And so on. When I'm on the air, my switchboard lights up like a fireworks castle on the 16th of September and my earphones hum with all these scared, lonely men.

As for me—I've always had my coffee without cream. I guess that's why I love girls whose skin is like maíz tostado. Brown girls know their power—they can be sweet as cajeta, yet sting like a whip. I even love those girls with fuzzy mustaches, those with gaps in their front teeth, the ones with red freckles, and las gorditas. They are all beautiful to me, they have given me their affection, and they've been cuates and camaradas. I have never thought of women as the enemy, as citadels to conquer, or the cause of ruin and damnation. I loved them all and they were all good. That's why I'm known as Doctor Corazón.

What gets me are men who don't take love seriously, the ones who say, "Hey Doctor Corazón, love is just an itch that must be scratched, hee, hee, hee." They think love doesn't hurt. But I tell you, love is like kneeling on broken glass. If you survive the pain you might be blessed with visions of heaven.

And tonight, on the Day of the Dead, Arturo's death, wrapped in the magenta-colored invitation, hurts like a nail through the sternum, like a hundred red devils are shoveling hot coals on my chest. But I'm cool. There's no crying allowed on the night of El Dia de los Muertos, because the dead will slip on the tears and won't find their way back. On the Day of the Dead laughter is the only cure for dying.

Before the mariachis start playing, La Betsy presents two belly dancers wrapped head to toe in transparent veils. They have silver bells fitted on their fingertips that tinkle like rain. Belts of silver coins gird their ample bellies, their jaws are outlined with white, their eyes with kohl, and their navels tattooed with violet wreaths exotic as the Kama Sutra. In the midst of the belly dancers' gyrations, a flamenco dancer skeleton jumps into it—his tight black pants showing off his pert ass and narrow waist, and his boot heels rapping a woodpecker's staccato on the floor. He is joined by a sultry, gypsy skeleton who follows the palmas while clutching a rose in her teeth. The gypsy skeleton embellishes her fancy zapateos with high kicks that reveal her honey-colored legs under ruffled polka-dotted skirts. Calaveras gather all wide-eyed around the dancers, stomping and clapping, keeping the fiesta jumping.

The Day of the Dead here is nothing like the one in Mexico, where children spread carpets of marigold petals on the streets so the dead can find their way home. Then the relatives throw a big party, get drunk and crack jokes to remind the dead of the fun they had in this world. Some families picnic all night in the cemeteries, on the graves, feasting with the dearly departed. In La Mission the celebration starts with a capitán of danza blowing a conchshell trumpet, the hoarse notes rising to the stars. We have Aztec dancers, samba dancers and puppeteers. Here we celebrate death with laughter and music. And that's how it should be, homey. Give me a drink of Gusano Rojo with a pinch of salt. I'll sing Mexican ballads all night, and eat pan de muerto—skeleton shaped bread—to mock La Pelona, let her know I don't give a fat chíngaso about her grip on my greñas. And when my time comes, serenade me with mariachis, build me an altar and spare me the tears.

†

When the mariachis take a break I step out to the patio, anxious to smoke a Delicado. You think I'm going to watch my health on the Day of the Dead? Don't be absurd. Tonight I want to tempt foxy Ms. Death, make her want me between her legs, crave me like I crave this tobacco. That's just how it is—ashes to ashes. Our lives a plucked guitar string, one brief note swallowed by the cosmos. Arturo's moment has come and gone. Same with the Brown Buffalo, Oscar Zeta Acosta, a writer who yanked me into the picture when I didn't know my destiny. Gone too is Tomás Rivera, Ricardo Sánchez, and José Antonio Burciaga,

Chicano writers, guitar strumming calaveras now, and I miss them all.

†

Back in the fiesta latintechno is blaring out of speakers hidden in two giant papier mâché skulls, one says Dot, the other, Com. All the calaveras are clacking bones, bumping and grinding to the music. A calavera Zapata is shaking it up with a calavera Frida. A zoot-suiter is swinging with his mamásota, their bones bright with neon paint. ¡Qué lucas! Two women calaveras are into a wild disco mambo—the butch has geometric designs tattooed on her biceps, a silver ring through her septum; the femme is sexy in latex dress and combat boots. Day of the Dead has room for everyone.

The music switches to tango and a merry calavera widow in a slinky black gown wants to dance with me. Why not? But I'm not fooled by the big smile behind the sequined black veil. I know it's Agapito Manglar, who runs a dance studio on 17th Street. But I tango with the transvestite widow anyway, dip her low, letting her white frizzy hair nearly sweep the floor. She kicks one leg up around my ear, pointing her silver shoes at the papel picado streamers, and her gown falls down the full length of her sheer black stockings. For a moment we're frozen in this pose, two calaveras wrapped around a tango. Then I glide the widow through the next step while the moody bandoneon fills the loft with music, sweet as a first kiss. Man, it's like a foreign movie I've seen somewhere. When the music stops we untangle our legs. Agapito winks at me and sashays off to nibble candy skulls with a Carmen Miranda calavera wearing a hat full of bones and bananas.

I go over to the altar where the burning copal unwinds a funnel of smoke. I drop a handful of fresh copal beads into the censer, and as the white smoke unfurls Arturo's face appears, his wispy goatee. In the days after the earthquake in Mexico City my sister Meche and I lived with Arturo's familia in San Angel. Arturo and I are the same age and when we were seven we shared our first Delicado. Later, when we were thirteen, he turned me on to peyote and I turned him on to Lorca. We roller coasted through the gates of perception—heaven and hell—apprentice brujos reciting saetas, our mescalito-lit eyes hurling sparks bright as roman candles. The next time I saw him we'd turned nineteen, and Arturo's eyes were as yellowed as a Mexico City sunset. His teeth were stained, his thumb pad singed a nicotine brown. I still remember his confession: "We were all there in Tlatelolco when the grenadiers began shooting. I escaped by hiding in a doorway. But some of my cuates were killed, others got ten years in Lecumberri."

In the aftershock of the student massacre in Tlatelolco, paranoia followed him like hungry dogs. He'd become a longhaired, bearded teporocho wandering the alleys of Tepito, a devotee of William S. Burroughs, a beat hipster of la capirucha. I dragged him out of La Capital, away from his tecato connections, and we hopped a train to Vera Cruz, where we hid out for two months in cheap hotels. I nursed him with rum and yesca while he weaned himself from carga, shooting smaller and smaller doses till he ran out of needles. Then he snorted till his stash was gone. With night sweats and vomit and tears, he finally kicked the gorilla off his back. He later claimed I saved his life.

In Vera Cruz we practically lived in palm-thatched bars called palapas, surrounded by the cawing of seabirds. Every sunset this trio, two guys on guitars and one on maracas, gathered around us. Their raw, sea-wind cracked voices were dipped in sentiment, pure as a straight shot of añejo tequila. We always requested "Camino de Guanajuato" because of the lyrics. And we'd always join in on the chorus—cantando con toda el alma— "No vale nada la vida/ La vida no vale nada." Life is worth nothing, nothing is worth life.

Each night we explored the cabarets in town and drank bottles of rum with mulata rumberas and jarocho musicians. Once, about 2 a.m. we even rang the buzzer at Agustín Lara's house, but the famous musician wasn't in. During those nights of Vera Cruz we philosophized about life, and about the women we wanted to love a lifetime. All melancholy with tequila, Arturo said: "One good woman is all I want, but all I find are the bad ones." I laughed and said, "You'll find her before you die." But he never did. At nineteen our future seeemed so far away we had nothing to fear. We didn't realize then that this was as good as it would ever get.

Several years later, the summer we turned twenty-five, Arturo invited me to scale Citlaltepetl, an 18,000 foot peak in Puebla. On the first day we climbed past the temperate heights, the region where nopales grow on the rocky skirts of the mountainside. The second day we rested on a ledge several thousand feet up, the view straight down a rocky cliff. The higher elevations are mostly hard-packed rock, without trails, but Arturo always found a way through gorges I thought uncrossable. When we camped at night the sky was lit with stars, and the nocturnal screeching of a thousand unseen beasts kept us awake.

On the third day of our ascent Arturo led our approach to the summit. I was following behind some ten feet when a blast of wind literally blew me off the trail and I was hurled down an embankment, granite scrapping my face and chest. A thin ledge just barely halted my fall before a steep drop. I froze on the rim of that abyss not daring to breathe, my heart bursting with fear. "Don't move," Arturo shouted, "I'm coming for you." Then he removed his pack and crawled on his stomach toward me, an inch at a time. He seemed to take a hundred years to cover those thirty feet. When he was close enough he stretched out his hand and we gripped each other's wrists and held on. If we slipped, we wouldn't hit the ground for maybe six or seven seconds. That's a long time for your life to flash before you. But he pulled me up, and as I crawled away my boots knocked loose some rocks that rolled over the edge and disappeared from sight.

Shaky and sweat-soaked, I climbed back to the trail. We'd come so far that we never mentioned turning back. I wiped the blood from my face with some canteen water and we kept going. An hour later when we finally stood on the peak of Citlaltepetl, our lungs were screaming for air and our eyes bursting with icy tears. From where we stood we could see the valley of Oaxaca; it looked like a brown soup bowl. We could see all the way to Vera Cruz even, the blue gulf like a promise of life. Together, standing side by side on those awesome heights, we threw our arms out to the Mexican sun, feeling all the power in the world, like demigods, scratched and bloodied but invincible, for a brief moment believing we would live forever.

†

I splash some Gusano Rojo mezcal in front of La Betsy's altar, an offering, an ofrenda for the spirits. May they help us keep our rituals, our customs, and our barrio alive. As I drink my way to a meeting with the gusano in the bottle, I toast Arturo and his other life. Only Gusano Rojo Mezcal goes down like maguey honey, tastes of Mexican earth after a summer shower. La Betsy's boyfriend, the orange-wigged calavera priest, comes around with the tray again. A plastic skeleton swings merrily from his neck and dangles over the candy craniums. He shoves the tray at me and says, "Come on vato, te vez un poco muerto, or better said, te vez demasiado vivo, já, já, já." You really need your friends with you on the Day of the Dead. This time under the sugar skull that says Selena, I find one with purple curlicues that spells out my name—Reymundo. Sugar rubies fill the eye sockets, blue sprinkles decorate the jaw. Beautiful. A satin ribbon under the candy skull says it all:

Tus besos me matan, your kisses kill me. With the last hit of Gusano Rojo Mezcal I wash down the sugar cranium, and the worm sticks to the side of the bottle refusing to slip into my mouth.

It's ten to midnight and I can feel Arturo nearby, waiting in the wings to make his entrance. I arrange his photo on the altar, next to the other photos and offerings, and I recall his contagious laugh. I strike a match to a candle, place the flame in front of Arturo's image. Because I love life. Because I laugh at death. To remember is to live again, my brother. I live for both of us now, you and me together, in this world and the next.

The music and laughter swirl around me like a Ferris wheel of brightly colored lights. I look around at all the skeletons having fun and from the shadows a stunning calavera appears, breathtaking in shimmery sequined dress, long black gloves, diamond bracelets dripping from her wrists. Her hourglass figure beautiful as all sin. She catches me staring and flashes a sexy smile, classical and sensuous and I smile back. The calavera winks, then beckons me with a bony finger as her red painted lips are mouthing the words, "Hey, come on, let's make it tonight." But I shake my head and smile at La Pelona. Not just yet flaca cabrona, I still have many battles to fight. So I turn my back on luscious Ms. Death, at least for now. Instead I warm my hands over the candles on the altar, those colored-flames still flickering, being consumed by their own energy, releasing memories and visions as they go on burning, lighting up the night.

# BARRIO LOTTO

Money's been the worry ever since when, so what else is new? Some time ago, I, Toño Tenorio, used to manage a little bar in La Mission. But since it closed I have been slaving for the Municipal Railway, taking abuse from every bastard with a buck to ride the bus. I've had coffee splashed on me, I've been spat upon, been beaten, been robbed. I still have a bump on my head from a bicycle chain, a gift from a gang-banger. One time a degenerate maniac whipped out his bony thing right there on my bus, and pissed in front of a group of horrified nuns. I tell you I could write a story, a whole book of crazy stories about life driving a bus. And I may have to, since a single paycheck— for Gina, Junior, me, and the twins we're expecting—just ain't making it.

I share my fortune with Gina, she's the sugar in my life, sweet and dark as guarapo syrup. Gina's so big these days her belly button looks like a thumb. A fat red accusing thumb. Doctor says it's twins. Maybe triplets. I don't know how to hang with that. We Mexicans have a saying: "Every baby comes with its own taco." But I wonder. Ever since Gina quit her job as a discrimination investigator for the government, our rent's been late. She quit because her boss, an expert in mental cruelty named Tiffany Fang, kept discriminating against her. If you were Latino, Black, Asian, Native American, Northern European, Ukranian, or any race at all, if you were male, female, overweight or a little on the thin side, if you were lesbian, gay, asexual, or if you didn't kowtow every morning when passing Kommandant Fang's office, she made your life a slow torture, Death by a Thousand Cuts.

Gina is Puerto Rican, island born, and raised by her very own nanny in the ritzy El Condado District of San Juan, but now she clips coupons and shops at the canned goods store. If a can of black beans has survived a train wreck or has fallen off a semi barreling down 101, if it's dented and smashed, Gina will track it down for two-thirds off the regular price. Still, at the end of the month, we're always down to zero dollars and I have to pick through my pockets for nickels and dimes.

My sugar used to have hair down to her waist. She'd wear it in plaits, French braids, cornrows, double loops over her ears, or she'd just let it hang naturally in thick wavy curls. Women would stop her on the street and want to know where she got her perm done. Gina'd laugh 'cause that was her natural God-given hair. I don't know why she cut it, a fit of depression I guess.

And what can I say about Junior? Two years old and he looks like a Mayan Gerber baby—long eyes, high forehead, big pansa. He chews everything that falls into his hands. Starting with his toys, then on to whatever's on the floor, especially paper. My son's a gourmet of paper. Tears it up and—there it goes—into his mouth. Sometimes he doesn't even bother tearing it, tries to eat it whole like a pizza. He must be on a mission to find the best tasting paper—bags, receipts, newspapers—you name it. You should see the faces he makes afterwards, crinkles his eyes and sticks out his tongue. Cracks you up. I guess the sports section doesn't make such a groovy lunch.

◆

Gina used to have this "gift," I called it. She'd mention rain and ten minutes later the abuela of all storms would come pounding your face. Knew her horoscope before she read it. Even the telenovelas, with their complicated twists and counter-plots, were no mystery. She'd know a month in advance how the love triangle in "Volver a Empezar" would turn out, and that would kill it for her.

One Saturday I had the TV going, my used black-and-white I have propped up on two milk crates. It was my day off, and I had settled into my genuine imitation leather La-Z-Boy I bought at Goodwill the last time I had money. I was nursing a cold Tecate, with salt and lime, the poor man's margarita. My ashtray was filled with crushed butts I meant to recycle into hand-rolled cigarettes. Times were tough. The Giants were down by three in the bottom of the ninth, two outs, bases loaded, and the batter's a rookie just up from Phoenix, filling in for their star outfielder out with a broken wrist.

Just then Gina comes by with Junior and says to me, "Toño, come with me to the Pak n' Save." And I say, "Sugar, this game's not over," and run my hand down the nice curve of her hip, 'cept now the curve is wider 'cause she's due any day. Gina sits on the armrest and yawns, "Boring."

Like grocery shopping is lion hunting. When the count reached 2 and 1 she bounced Junior on her lap, closed her eyes, and predicted, "He's going to hit a hummer."

"You mean a homer."

"Whatever. I can feel it."

"Sugar, it's his first at bat in the majors."

"Do I care?"

"Two bucks says you're wrong."

"How 'bout going with me to the Pak n' Save? You pack."

On the next pitch the rookie blasted a line drive that sailed past the left fielder's outstretched glove and cleared the fence by inches. A delirious roar rumbled from the TV. I jumped up and shouted, "Aaaw right!" Gina just laughed and bounced Junior on her hip. I tell you she was plugged into the future's very own special channel.

What I'm saying is there's all kinds of people. Some, like Gina, have their magic, a sixth sense, un sentido. They dream in technicolor and their dreams speak to them. They see omens in the flight of birds. They read the future like you and I read the want ads. They're born with this gift, how else would they have it? You can't find it on the street or your corner church, can't buy it a candle shop, though people try.

◆

When Gina finally quit work, I supported her decision. We were already on rice and beans, so I said, "We'll go on bread and water." Who needs discrimination on the job, anyway?

Gina was two weeks overdue with Junior and feeling

low, so I said, "What the heck, let's do it. Let's get married."
We married without a wedding ring, couldn't afford one,
and my friend, Tito Castaneda, the notary public at
Economy Weddings, didn't care. I slipped him a ten spot so
he could stamp the certificate and give us new titles, wife
and husband. Esposa y esposado. Gina never complained;
she's a good sport when her friends flash diamond rings
that could put your eye out.

My sugar doesn't care for sex right now, too uncomfortable she says, and with those two or three kids inside her
kicking like a world-class soccer team, I can't argue. But
the other night, sitting on the La-Z-Boy, she kinda absent-
mindedly said, "No more kids after this." I didn't look up. I
just kept massaging her swollen ankles, massaging her
feet. Gina has the prettiest toes, they're like little Tootsie
Rolls I want to pop in my mouth. Sometimes she wears silver rings on them and I'll paint her toenails dark red,
makes her feel glamorous as a movie star. But she went on
in that same tone. "One of us, either you or I, will have to
take the cruelest cut," and I knew Gina was right about
that cut and this knowledge settled in my heart, heavy as
original sin.

◆

I learned about Gina's magic powers when we went to the
racetrack at Bay Meadows. I was with Mundo and some of
the guys from work. We were pouring over the racing
form, smoking some powerful Humboldt stuff, and mark-
ing x's and o's beside each horse—comparing tip sheets,

calculating speed ratings, jockeys, trainers, past performances. Does the horse have bad habits like giving up half way through the race? Who's the foal mare? What about the stud? After a while all these marks looked like Egyptian hieroglyphs written by illiterate mule drivers.

My first three bets ran out of the money. Gina'd been watching my madcap calculations and decided to bet five dollars. So I showed her the program, the race was a $2,500 claimer, six furlongs, three-year-olds and up, non-winners in the past year. These horses were running downwind of the glue factory. She looked through the program and found one she liked, Miss Mary. The name reminded Gina of her dear nanny, María Santa María, the santera from Arecibo, or someplace, who'd raised her in old San Juan. I looked in the form and shook my head. Miss Mary, a six-year-old mare, had not won in three seasons, twenty-four races in a row, had not even placed since she broke her maiden on the fair circuit. Her last time out, Miss Mary finished a distant thirty-seven lengths back. This horse was practically dead on its hooves, an embarrassment to its breed. We went to the paddock to make sure Miss Mary had four legs. OK, she had four legs but the poor thing was limping. "No good, can't you see," I told Gina. But my sugar bet her five dollars because she liked the name. Can you believe it? The horse was 99-1 when the race started.

So the flag goes up, the buzzer rings, and the horses are off. At the quarter-pole they're all bunched up in the middle. By the half, four are running together, Miss Mary right with them on the rail, her tail straight out like a wire.

Coming around the far turn she stuck her nose in front, and heading down the stretch it's Miss Mary all the way, running like she hears the glue wagon hauling ass behind her. The crowd is screaming like crazed banshees and I don't have to tell you who won.

Gina cashed in 540 mangoes. I had to shake my head. The next day she starts predicting the weather like she has a secret satellite in orbit. We used to joke about it, not knowing what a real gift she had. Until we started betting on it.

One morning she dreamed about hitting the lotto. I was still in bed, just waking up, when she told me about it. "I was sitting by a pool and all these waiters in white jackets were bringing me champagne and I'd say, 'Oh, I have enough. Gracias.' But they kept on pouring and pouring. Ay, Papí, I wish you could have been in the dream with me."

Her dream bothered me, 'cause I wasn't in it, and I guess I spaced out on the bus that day, nearly ran over a kid and his dog, missed the kid by an inch.

But Gina took the dream as an omen—after all, she's familiar with intuition. She got it stuck in her head to go after the big one, ¡Zas!, six numbers and our worries would be over. I warned her, "Don't mess with the magic." The first time she played she missed by two numbers. She picked up her consolation $50 and was hooked. Pretty soon it's $5 here, another $10 there. Every Tuesday, Thursday, and Saturday I'm at the liquor store buying tickets with different combinations, and blowing ten, fifteen bucks a pop. Then I found out she'd been to visit Sister Lola on Mission Street, you know the place. The orange neon hand in the window—FORTUNES TOLD. KNOW YOUR LUCKY NUMBER. I asked Gina about Sister Lola, but she shrugged it off, said she was looking for tarot cards to send her nanny back in P.R. I was still suspicious. I mean, if Sister Lola has an inside line to the future, why doesn't she play the Lotto instead of selling the winning number for ten bucks? My poor Gina, sometimes she'll cry out in the middle of the night— "The 7, the 7." Or maybe—"15, the 15!" Then I can't go back to sleep waiting for her to shout the next number so I can write it down, just in case. You never know.

◆

We live in the heart of La Mission, an old Victorian flat on 24th and Valencia, above Muddy's Café. Kristin, who runs the café, is a goddess who brings me to life every morning. Soon as I walk in she'll say, "Double espresso, right?" Makes me feel good, like I'm a valued customer. If I have a day off, I sit in the café and read about all the lofts going up and the evictions of poor people, or crime and violence in the city, which is the same thing. One car stolen every fifteen seconds in this town. Good thing I can't afford one. Can't afford a loft either. I can barely afford the flat we live in. Not that it's anything fancy with that crack in the wall that looks like the Amazon River. And every winter the crack gets bigger, like there's more water flowing in the Amazon or something. From our flat we hear everything that goes on in the street. If people are arguing we can tell if they're from El Salvador or Oaxaca by their accents, or when the low riders come by blasting their hip-hop, our windows rattle like the bass was in our kitchen.

Every morning I see the Red Man hanging around Muddy's. That's what I call him, the Red Man. Dresses all in red, red pants, red shoes, red hat, and get this, even paints his face red. Looks like Dali on acid. But I say hello to him anyway. I like the way he dresses how he wants, paints his face if he wants. He's harmless, a walking art piece. Brings a smile to my face. If I'm due to pull out a bus, I finish my coffee and walk over to Potrero Yard. At that hour Mission Street is filled with women sleeping in doorways, on newspapers. The old men usually take the benches. I know this is the richest country in the world, and it's sure not right. Seems there should be enough to go around. What I don't understand is how this country came to be so poor. I mean this is a major cosmopolitan city, but the streets are filled with holes, no different from Tegucigalpa. And every day there's more wigged-out freaks on the buses, shoes unlaced, drool dripping from their mouths, tuning into radio waves from Mars. I get angry sometimes, but what good does it do?

When I'm nailed behind the wheel, for ten and twelve hour days, I think it must run in the family. My old man drove buses for thirty-five years in Mexico City, the Tacuba route. My grandfather was the engineer on Pancho Villa's train. Man, does he have stories. So ever since I was a kid growing up in La Mission I've wanted to be a bus driver. When Mr. Jones, the counselor at Mission High School, would ask my career plans, I had a one word answer— "Buses." He'd reply by forcing some real foul smelling air through his nicotine stained teeth, and jotting down something in his pad. I never knew what he was writing. I never even knew if he was listening. Sometimes I felt like shouting, "Babes! Boobs! Buses!" just to shake him up. But I never did. Even back in high school I knew mine was the life of a worker bee.

The passengers are the one that make you or break you. One time it was pouring buckets so I could barely see through the windshield. The bus was packed with folks going home to the projects, and everyone of them in a bad mood. This was an express run and I was making just one out of every five stops. I'm flying down Geneva over by the Cow Palace—I swear I didn't hear a buzzer ring—when this Samoan woman pushes her way to the front and glares down at me. She looked mean as the starting left tackle for the 49rs. On defense. She goes, "Alamalakalakahani," or something like that. "Say what?" I said, not wanting to take my eyes off the road under those conditions. But I see out the corner of my eye that she's about ready to slam an umbrella over my head. Then she screamed in my face, "You miss my stop!"

I hit the brakes so hard I made more introductions than a swinger's party. The bus came to a dead halt right there in the middle of traffic and I opened the door. The 300-pound tackle stomped off, each step of hers down the stepwell shaking the bus like Godzilla. My ears were burning with all kinds of moans and curses coming from people untangling themselves on the floor, and the Samoan lady turns around and shouts at me, "You no good bus driver!"

✦

After a bad day driving I drop by the Slow Club—and sit in the dark café, staring at a pint of Pilsner, too tired to think, but I'm thinking this: My whole life? All of it? The big boys squeeze the juice out of a man and spit out the pits. They make lemonade out of you and before you know it, you're fertilizing a manicured lawn somewhere, and that's it. What's it all supposed to mean? It doesn't seem possible my life is about this. I'm meant for better things, I know it. And Junior, what's his fate? And the twins or triplets we're expecting?

Then I think of the crazies on my bus, living without two cents worth of luck, and I see luck is just a matter of degrees. Once, when I was young, a viejito told me that luck has a secret name, luck is not its real name at all, and whoever knows the true name will have happiness in buckets. And for a shot of tequila he'd tell me the true name of luck. But I must have put the name in a vault without a combination 'cause the next morning I forgot it. And no matter how hard I've tried to call it up—something like Anaromana—or close to it, I never get it right. I know 'cause my luck's never changed. So there's no escape for me, and most days I just swallow the bitter brew of my fate and dream of some beach where the beer is always cold.

But responsibility spins a man like a top. So instead of running off to the South Pacific and living naked in the wild with a tropical babe, I go home and avoid the mail, just dump it in a kitchen drawer with the rest of the unpaid bills. I greet Gina like a thief, a quick kiss and I'm out of her face. I put on my sunglasses, plug in my headphones, the volume on max, pop a cut-rate cold one, and slump down in the torn-up La-Z-Boy, frying my brains to Tower of Power, "Diamonds Sparkling in the Sand," or Santana's old rock music, "Black Magic Woman." If my nephew has dropped off a joint, I fire up, play some reggae. I like Bob Marley, no one better than that Rastafari for turning despair into inspiration.

After one of those bad days Gina avoids me till I'm more or less mellowed out. That woman has a heart big as a bus barn. Over dinner, I usually ask how's the Lotto—any luck? Sometimes she'll mention some new combination she's working on, or she'll say, "Next week, the planets will favor us." In the beginning I kinda believed her, but when she started bringing home candles and powders from that botanica on Valencia Street, you know, that disco-magic, aerosol spray of Siete Poderes, I knew the bad luck curse of the working class had struck again.

I think it was cutting her long hair into tight curls that did it, or being pregnant, or both, but ever since she's been making babies in triplicate, she's lost her magic touch. She has to look at the calendar to see what day comes next. Last week she didn't pick a number in ten Lotto tickets. She doesn't want to stop, but I tell her it's time to quit, should have never profaned the magic that way. Now it's just bad luck, broken luck, or no luck at all—una suerte salada. Luck without a name.

+

What bugs me is how the Lotto is dangled like a golden taco in front of poor Latin people. At work you see all these Spanish Lotto ads plastered on the sides of the buses. I knew this mechanic, Teofilo Sánchez, who'd blow every paycheck on a roll of tickets. He hit nothing but a few teasers and after several years lost his family over his gambling, then lost his house, went partially insane with the frustration, shot his boss at work. Blew the guy's kneecap off.

But not everyone's been hurting. Take Jimmy Summore. Here's a bro, half-Puerto Rican, dark as a double espresso and twice as bitter, so you know he's lived the other side. Summore made supervisor at the Municipal Railway, drove a shiny white Cadillac, only Puerto Rican had a car without a dent. Summore was a real company man. Even posted his own set of rules in the gilley room: No cussing; No gambling at any time; Radios off by eight p.m. Like Muni was his own private property. We just laughed at the Summore Rules. You won't find one guy that's worked for him, not a one, who has a good word to say about the man. Our own kind is often the worst.

And he loved yelling at operators. One time, ol' Jules, he's from New Orleans, was doing overtime and pulled in the lot to take a quick 702. Had to leak. He's not in there but a minute or two, but Summore sees the bus parked, runs out and starts hollering like there's a fire. When ol' Jules comes out, Summore screams in his face. Jules is a twenty-eight-year veteran of the buses, he's a little bowlegged but his heart is straight, and he tells Summore, "If you don't shut up, I'm gonna take me another 702." Jules was running late or I think he would have popped Summore one. The point is you don't talk that trash to hard working folks.

Summore even suspended me once, gave me time at the beach, as we say. It was last year right before the holidays. I'd been on the buses a few years, and never wore a uniform. I'd wear the Muni shirt with my jeans. Nobody cared except Summore. Day before Christmas he stopped me from pulling out on the Geary line. Told me to shut the bus down and brake it. He wanted to see me in his office. As I'm going in, the union rep is coming out, and he tells me, "Summore has the order written up, there's nothing we can do, Toño. Just take it." A three-day suspension. Merry Christmas. Ho, ho, ho.

So you can imagine my surprise when a couple of weeks ago I see Summore's picture in the paper. Turns out the guy's been stealing from the fare box. They'd been watching him for months. He'd been going in at night, riffling the fare boxes before the morning crews came in to do the counting. They found duffel bags stuffed with quarters in his house. Must have weighed tons. They fired his ugly ass in a minute. No tears shed around the bus yard I can tell you that. When you steal from working people, literally stick your fist in and take, then I guess there's nothing lower.

So guess what happened today? I'm out on the avenues doing an express trip and who do I see running to catch my bus, but Mister Summore. He's hauling a briefcase, tie flapping, and wearing a shit-eating grin. Looked like he was late for a job interview. I let him get right up to the door, let him see who was driving, and that I was wearing jeans—then I slammed the door in his face. I punched the transmission into gear, pushed the pedal to the metal, and left him stewing in a cloud of white exhaust fumes. I could see him in my rear-view mirror shaking a fist and cussing me out. And that just made my day. I said hello to every passenger at the next stop and smiled all the way to the end of the line.

I couldn't wait to tell Gina about it. For the first time in months I came home in a halfway decent mood, not like some kind of werewolf. But I walk in and, hey, what's going on? All the lights were off. Three gold candles were lit on the kitchen table and the scent of arroz con pollo filled our two room flat like a blessed miracle. Made me want to faint with hunger. There was even a chilled bottle of wine on the table, the ten-dollar-a-bottle kind, not that cheap swill we're used to from the canned food outlet, you know, the $1.99 stuff from the ghetto part of the vineyard.

Junior, he's just starting to walk. He's by the milk crates under the TV, stuffing some paper in his mouth as usual. What a funny kid, I think to myself. Then Gina jumps out from a closet and nearly gives me a heart attack. She flings her arms around me, and hugs me as tight as she can with what's between us. "So what's up?" I ask. Wouldn't you?

I knew this was going to be good because I'd never seen her so ecstatic. Not even on our wedding night.

She screamed, "I did it! I did it! I hit the Lotto!" The words rang in my ears like a trolley bell clanging.

"We did what?" I said. I couldn't believe it. "How much?"

"Twenty thousand coconuts. Twelve after taxes. Ave María dios mío."

I kissed her about thirty times. "Oh sugar, sugar, sugar. You're absolutely luscious. Oh, yes, yes, yes." Kiss, kiss, kiss.

We hugged and screamed and kissed and cried. Never felt so high, like a dozen buses were lifted off my neck. Finally, a chance in a lifetime.

I uncorked the bottle, poured us a big glass of wine.

"So let's see this ticket." I was picturing a sunset in San Juan. How the relatives will love me now.

"It's right over here by the TV," she says.

Only it's not there now.

"I swore that's where I put it. I'm positive," she says.

"You wouldn't joke about this, would you?"

"Not on your life."

So we start searching for it. Everywhere. Desperate. Double check all her pockets, check the trash, check the floor on our hands and knees. Check the trash again.

Then it comes to me. A sinking feeling in my stomach, like when I was a kid and had to go in for a tetanus shot. I picked Junior up and looked into his long brown innocent eyes. The veins in my temples were suddenly throbbing.

I spoke to him in a friendly fatherly voice. "Junior, let Papí see what you got in your mouth."

My curly-haired, Mexi-Rican Gerber baby just shook his head.

"Aw come on, open for Papí."

Nothing doing. So I gently stuck a finger in his little

mouth, and pushed past his four baby teeth gnawing at my knuckle with all the hunger of his two-year old life, till I felt something back in there all kinda mooshy and chewed up.

I turned to Gina, my heart pounding like a racehorse. "I . . . found . . . something . . . ."

She was praying with her palms together and her eyes aimed at the crack in the ceiling that looks like the Amazon. Then I pulled the wet lump out of Junior's mouth and heard Gina whisper, "Ave María dios mío." But I kept my eyes on Gina and she kept her eyes on me and we exchanged looks only the truly desperate understand.

# LUCKY ALLEY

I never understood why they called this graffiti-scarred alley "lucky." Still the same as when I lived here—littered with abandoned shopping carts, broken-spring couches, pools of dirty oil and a million shards of glass. Beer swigging vatos dealing dope from parked cars, and piss smell so thick that the stray cats under stoops look like they're holding their breath. At sundown, dust motes swirling in the hazy light between Victorian-age tenements make even the air seem dangerous, and you know nothing but bad luck is going to happen here.

Passing by Lucky Alley always reminds me of Catarino Maraña—drove a pearl-white sports car, a '60 Triumph with canvas top. I sold him the top after wrecking my own Triumph. Funny that when I think of other people's fate I think of my own. During my bad days I totalled my share of cars. The last one, a signal-red TR3 roadster, happened one Saturday night when I turned, piss-drunk, into Lucky Alley and never saw the streetlight step in front of me—I woke up in General Hospital, an intern stitching my forehead like he was mending a sock, leaving this crescent scar to remind me.

I wrecked the Triumph after an all night borrachera with my girlfriend Luz. She had finally agreed to move into my studio apartment, 13 Lucky Alley, and we'd been celebrating with shots of tequila and beer chasers. So when I left her house the stairs seemed more slanted than usual, and it took me an hour to find my keys, though they were in my pocket all along. Her face was the last thing I flashed on before the pinwheel of nausea exploded in my head, then, like in a movie—everything faded to darkness.

Luz is the most exquisite woman in La Mission, her brows thick as charcoal smudges and black as a pampas night. She's Argentine and can't stand stereotypes—hates tangos, beefsteaks, Evita, and the films of Armando Bo and Isabel Sarli. Peron kicked her family out of Argentina, and she's lived her whole life here in La Mission, like everyone else I know. She loves cinema more than anything. But I'd been into movies way before I met her.

She appeared one day at the Ribeltad Vorden—that place across Precita Park where I tended bar—sporting a cocky red beret and a light meter around her neck, asking if she could film the poets, locos, revolutionaries, and anarchists that hang out there. Why not? I said, while pouring a foamy pitcher of Anchor Steam for a crew of working men.

She loaded a cannister of film in her Bolex and told me about her movie on La Mission—she wanted to get the truth down about this barrio, warts, junkies, and all. I slid the pitcher down the plank and said beers were on the house when she finished. It's hard for people to relax around a camera, so I liked how she approached the junkies nodding in the park and the drunken poets reading on the little stage, even me, pouring a draft, without making us feel like we were freaks in a circus. Before she packed her gear I asked for her number, and a week later took her to La Taqueria Maya, then a double-feature at the New Mission, *El Santo Contra las Momias de Guanajuato,* and another one I forget. El Santo, my boyhood hero, the Mexican wrestler with silver mask and tights. In one scene he's driving a white Corvette when seven thugs jump him in an alley. The bad guys attack with 2 x 4s, chains, and clubs while El Santo fights back with all his champion wrestler moves, flying kicks and all. Cut to the next scene—El Santo is sitting down to a formal dinner wearing a tux and his silver mask and you never find out how he escaped. We laughed, it was so bad.

Later that night we wound up at my studio in Lucky Alley, a red candle lit for atmosphere. We were fooling around on the mattress, I had her blouse off, my right hand on her left breast, when she stopped me with a question.

"Would you ever lie to me?"

The candlelight was so perfectly romantic, it was like in a foreign movie, something by Lina Wertmuller.

"Never," I said, and meant it.

She said, "Not telling is also lying."

My tongue was already dipping into her navel, and her words were lost on me. I fumbled with unzipping her pants and grunted what sounded like agreement, and she said, "Because I'll never forgive a lie."

That was the start of our affair.

✦

I didn't know Catarino in those days I was wrecking cars, but he lived on Folsom Street, around the corner from Lucky Alley. I met him a few months after my last wreck. I'd gone to a foreign-film distributor in North Beach to rent *Mexico, the Frozen Revolution*, about government corruption after the 1910 Revolution. I wanted to impress Luz by starting a film series in La Mission, a *cine* club, to bring underground classics like *Memorias de Subdesarollo* and *Reed-Mexico Insurgente*, something really political to the barrio, an alternative to the telenovela mentality.

Catarino was pacing back and forth in the snazzy offices of Revolutionary Films, rapping a mile a minute on the phone. He mouthed the words around a cigarette stub and exhaled the smoke through his nose like Bogart in *The Treasure of the Sierra Madre*. His thick mustache was waxed and the tips curled to a fine point, like the bad guy in a silent movie. A giant orange and brown poster of Zapata covered the wall behind him. Catarino cupped the receiver on his thigh to greet me, pushed his wire-rim glasses back with one finger, loosened his tie, then asked the blonde receptionist to send a memo. He set the receiver down while he stuffed an envelope with publicity flyers and explained the hardships of the movie business. The problem was cash flow, he said. In three seconds he returned to his phone conversation like I wasn't there. I barely got a word in before he rushed out for lunch telling the receptionist he'd taken a twenty from petty cash.

♦

My father started me on movies. His addiction goes back to the first reels carried on muleback over narrow trails to his small town in Jalisco. Silent movies were screened at dusk on a cotton sheet hung in the open-air plaza, the projector's flickering light blinding the fruit bats swooping through the royal palms. Later, in Mexico City, the classic leading men of the golden age of Mexican cinema were his idols, in particular that scowling, dark-eyed, film-noir legend, Pedro Arméndariz. My father fashioned his life after those Mexican matinee idols—rigid in his honor, brave around men, courteous to women—except he doesn't sing or ride a horse. And if a woman leaves you for another man, burn every scrap of her memory like Cortés torching Tenochtitlán. That's Mexican movies for you. Remember the one in which María Félix tells Pedro Arméndariz she's been raped by a troop of soldiers? He cocks an eyebrow at her like a pistol and says, "Why didn't you let them kill you instead?" Hmmm. That was me. Until I met Luz. Then I learned that love and honor are not like in the movies.

The third *cine* club night at the Precita Community Center I sneaked out to call Luz and some sprockets tore on the film. By the time I heard the audience howling, several hundred feet of *Viva Zapata!* lay piled on the floor like black spaghetti. I refunded the gate to placate the mob. What money I had left went to pay for the damaged film. Somehow it didn't seem right to continue with the *cine* club, so I filed away the idea and chalked it up to experience.

✦

A couple of weeks after that fiasco, a noisy, pearl-white Triumph pulled up outside the Ribeltad Vorden. But a Triumph is not so cool without the top.

Right away I recognized Catarino when he slid up to the mahogany bar and ordered an Anchor Steam. I reminded him about Revolutionary Films and slipped him a draught on the house—but hell, that was usual for me. No one I knew ever went thirsty when I worked the plank.

Catarino grew up in El Paso where he learned early about fast women, good mota, and Johnny Law. Texas reform schools perfected his hustling and dealing. Then after a stint in Huntsville picking cotton for the Texas Rangers he came out to the coast and settled in La Mission. His voice was harsh as a rasp file, the words scraped from deep in his chest where the cigarette smoke collected. At thirty-seven he had fifteen years on me, he knew plenty about the movie business and spoke with authority about films, directors and life. You'd maybe not guess he'd spent ten years in the joint, but he had, for possession of heroin—a kilo and a half. When he told me I wasn't shook by it. Cat, as he liked to be called, never sat still, always moving around the bar, beer in hand, intense, ready to pounce. I liked that about him. You might call him a hustler, *vivo* my father would say—neither would be wrong.

I offered him the white canvas top of my Triumph, the only thing I salvaged when I wrecked in Lucky Alley. I asked a hundred for it, but took eighty and got fifty, the rest an I.O.U. that I still have in a drawer somewhere. That's when I learned Cat was often a little short, light in the wallet he'd say with a sly grin. Toño, who managed the Ribeltad and knew Cat well, liked to keep a check on him. He often told me: Forgive your friends their major sins but keep a limit on the tab.

A few weeks later, Revolutionary Films folded and Cat started hanging out more often at the Ribeltad. Those times when he appeared flushed with cash—I never asked where it came from since it wasn't my business—he always paid off his tab and left a nice tip.

One slow night Cat dropped by while I was behind the plank, the red neon Ribeltad sign lighting up the empty bar. I poured him a beer and asked how the Triumph was running, since I'd been missing my own. "Looks better with the top you sold me," he said, and before I could bring up the I.O.U, he asked me to join him in the storage room. Back there, among stacked beer cases, he fired up a fat joint. After a couple of tokes he laid two tickets on me for a special screening of Les Blank's *Chulas Fronteras*. "For the free beers, Mundo," he said. And high on that purple smoke, I figured Cat a vato who'd give you the last sip of beer in his mug.

A few nights later Cat dropped in near closing time and helped me shoo out the last drunks. I dimmed the bar lights so cruising cop cars wouldn't see us and, with the bar closed down, we drank for free and talked films—subversive and otherwise—*8½*, *The Damned*, *El Topo*. Cat's deep-set, beer-bottle-colored eyes, reflected the burning ember of his cigarette, and when we finally left near sunrise we were tight as partners in crime.

This became our ritual. Two, three times a week Cat would appear around closing hour, and after I'd shut down the plank we'd sit in the dark sharing pitchers of beer. One of those nights, well into our third pitcher, I'm not sure how the idea of leasing the York Theater on 24th Street in the heart of La Mission came up. The York had been closed for years, but as a kid just arrived from Mexico I'd spent many Saturdays mesmerized in the plush-velvet seats while Zorro outsmarted the bad guys, or green scaly monsters wracked havoc on the planet. During intermission I'd lean back in my seat and trace every curlicue on the plaster gold-leaf design that decorated the ceiling. To this day, the smell of roasting popcorn conjures up the York Theater and those childhood Saturday matinees.

At first I wasn't sure about the project, but little by little, night after night in the empty bar draining pitchers of Anchor Steam with Cat, he convinced me. The York Theater is an architectural gem, and a gala premier featuring the golden age of Mexican cinema, movies like *Los Olvidados, Nosotros los Pobres, La Mujer del Puerto*, could blow everyone away, have a tremendous impact, start a whole new trend in film appreciation.

Somehow Cat located the owner of the York, a guy in Hollywood named Brody, who wanted a five-grand deposit on a one-year lease. Cat said he had a thousand in cash, could I raise the rest? I had to think about this. Luz and I had struggled to save two grand to pay her last year's tuition at the Art Institute. We'd even thrown around the idea of a bigger place for us since my studio in Lucky Alley was now tightly crammed. So every Saturday we'd read the classifieds. We looked at some real dogs and some nice ones we couldn't afford.

Finally, Luz set her heart on a Victorian flat above Tede Wong's Chinese laundry on 24th and San Bruno. The walls needed serious paint, but it was big enough for an editing table in a corner of the living room. All we were waiting for was the word from Mr. Habib, the landlord, to tell us it was ours.

+

All this happened in the middle of a seven-year drought. Newspapers said the planets were lined up all wrong or something, and the Gods of Bad Luck owned the calendar. Every day the skies burned a pretty shade of industrial brown. Winters came dry as parchment, with no rains but a few pissy storms. And summers like tinder, radiators would suddenly blow, and a spark could incite riots. At night on 24th Street, young cholas in Daisy Dukes strolled the sidewalks, the half-moon of their nalgitas showing, and vatos cruised in low-riders, tooting on those insane car horns "La Cucaracha." And all the drunken fights at the Ribeltad. Some nights I even had to use the little bat behind the bar to keep the peace. Gunshots in Lucky Alley and around the corner keeping Luz and me awake till four in the morning sounded like the Wild West with Uzi's. And if it was quiet, we'd hear mice running between the walls, loud as horses. By the end of that summer I was burned out. I knew things had to change or I'd get my skull cracked one night trying to stop a fight at the Ribeltad or walking home through Lucky Alley.

But on those nights when I stayed late drinking with Cat, I'd come home to Lucky Alley with my head full of ideas about the York, and I'd lay awake thinking how to tell Luz. I already knew what she'd say. Luz is a food-on-the-table, the-bills-paid kind of woman. Don't come to her with get rich schemes 'cause she'll tell you every reason why they'll fail. She burns steady, just enough and every day; me—I fire up the middle and both ends. I guess our contradictions unite us.

So after wracking my brain for several nights I called this one alone—I figured better not give Luz a choice, just present her with the done deal. I withdrew our savings without telling her. Then to complete the deposit on the York I signed for the other two grand from a loan company at 22%. I'd never known a debt that big, and if you look at the loan papers you can see where my signature wavers off the dotted line.

Now you might think what I did was low and cold-blooded, but I did it for Luz, only she doesn't see it that way. Unless you've worked a job bartending, or waitressing, you have no idea of the desperation that fills your life, you dream of a way out, and to the drowning even straws look like ships to the rescue.

The next day Cat popped into the Ribeltad Vorden with ten crisp hundred-dollar bills, and I turned over my share in a white envelope. We called Brody from the bar phone and he agreed to fly in on Saturday to walk us through the theater and sign the papers. Cat said he'd get a cashier's check for Brody. We toasted to success with a pitcher of Anchor Steam, on the house.

The rest of the day I was so high I could barely eat. I was just bursting inside to tell Luz, 'cause I knew she was tired of La Rondalla, where she served drinks in a fluffy skirt and low-cut blouse. She was tired of the cheap tips and lewd comments. And her negatives piled in boxes. So at night while she was sleeping I was thinking of running the York, of that magic moment we'd throw open the doors for the grand premier and the house lights would dim, the credits come on, and the expectant faces light up. I even planned for Luz to show her own films, one of her cinema-verité black-and-whites that haunt you for days with their powerful images. Because that's the test of a great film— how much you remember days later. But film is also about forgetting, about sitting in a darkened theater losing yourself in those evanescent images, forgetting everything, even your betrayals. Your desgraciada suerte. You should see Luz's Super-8s, you can see she likes Shirley Clarke. They showed one last year at the Roxie, an interview with a woman who'd been waitressing twenty-seven years. The audience gave Luz a standing ovation. Luz still talks of making feature films, and she will, but right now she's editing commercials for Channel Five. She hates it, says she wants to do subversive work, not commercial shit.

◆

But as the week went on, Cat disappeared, and I grew tense as a death-row inmate waiting for a pardon. And each time I stole a look at Luz I felt ants in my stomach.

Thursday was my day off and Luz and I went to Dolores Park, then ate dinner at Los Panchos on Mission Street. When we came home early that evening, Lucky Alley was blocked off with police cars. I asked a cop what the trouble was and he said there'd been a shoot-out. Somebody killed. I didn't think twice about it, normal in my alley.

But I was quite edgy that night, anxious, feeling there was something wrong. I had to talk to Luz. She was at the editing machine set up on the kitchen table. Because of her negatives she kept the studio so clean you could eat off the floor, but for some reason there was a cucaracha poking two thin feelers around a can of film, unsure whether it should come out into the light. I had one eye on Luz, one eye on the cuca, but my mind on Cat.

Finally, like I'd just learned to talk, I blurted out to Luz where I'd put all our money. She looked up from the viewer. She thought I was kidding. "No," I said, "I'm serious as the Sixth Commandment." She stared at me like I'd burned her negatives, her eyes pinpoints of black light. "How could you without telling me?" is what she said. "And what makes you think you can trust Catarino?"

She must have seen my doubts, clear as a strip of film under light. But I kept talking about how things would take off for us, then I stopped. She had me pinned with those Argentine eyes of hers, her brows bunched together forming one solid wing across her forehead, but she wasn't seeing me, she was seeing her dreams of a degree slipping away like the twelve o'clock ferry to Sausalito.

Without saying another word she locked herself in the bathroom and wouldn't open the door, but I could hear her smashing things. I slumped in the kitchen, my scar throbbing like an open vein, feeling like I had slept with another woman, or worse, and nothing since has ever made me feel as bad.

I stared at the bubbled-up linoleum for a long time, traced the cracks across the kitchen wall. The sour odors in the woodwork we tried so hard to scrub away seemed to rise up and mock me. When the lousy cockroach finally made a dash across the kitchen table, I trapped it with my thumb and squashed it into the next world.

✦

I woke up in the morning on the couch, in a sour mood, a throbbing pain right behind my eyes. Toño, from the Ribeltad, was on the phone. He asked me to meet him at the Hall of Justice on 7th Street. Something urgent. He wouldn't talk about it till we were going down the hot, piss-smelling elevator to the morgue. At the mention of Catarino's name, my heart wrinkled up like an airless balloon.

A pale, maggoty-looking sheriff met us at the metal door of the morgue. For a quick second the chevrons on his arms looked like crossbones. We followed his dull footsteps to a walk-in freezer that smelled of chrome and formaldehyde. The frozen dead rested on gurneys, a tag wired around a big toe. The dead came in all the colors of the city—a homeless white woman, legs thick with varicose veins; a Chinese guy, emaciated, thin as a twig; a young black chick, still good-looking even in death. The sheriff paused before one of the gurneys and pulled back the white sheet, and there was Cat—dead and naked, one eye closed and one partly opened, staring at a movie only he could see. What were the credits on the big screen in the sky? Death had stripped away his cool-as-ice look and turned his face and chest a cement color. A smudge of gunpowder burned a little hole on his forehead like the dot on a question mark. Anger, rage, I don't know, made the scar on my forehead want to burst.

Can we identify the body? The keeper of the dead wants to know. It's Catarino all right, that's his mustache still waxed and curled, though the tips looked a bit singed. In a monotone voice the sheriff says that the District Attorney would be holding an inquiry, but this case was pretty much open-and-shut. Catarino and a partner were scoring some Mexican heroin, but it was a sting, the dealers undercover narcs. And there'd been a shoot-out.

There wasn't much I could do for Catarino. Pobrecito. Then I thought, why should I feel sorry for him when I have Luz and myself to feel sorry for? Then the anger came back, and I started thinking—Damn it, Cat, what were you doing? And what about your friends, did you think of them? Outrage pulled me one way, anger another, and the truth tore me down the middle.

Toño wanted to claim the body, but the sheriffs wouldn't release it till after the autopsy and the inquiry. They did turn over a manila envelope with Catarino's belongings—a wristwatch with a worn leather strap, an empty wallet, his wire-rim glasses with one lens busted.

I said good-bye to Toño in front of the Hall of Justice and walked to the bus stop. After the darkness of the morgue the daylight hurt my eyes and everything seemed so clear and transparent. Not a leaf stirred on the chestnut trees. Flocks of blackbirds perched on the telephone wires silent as mourners. And I wanted to hurl bricks at windows and kick every cop that passed.

Days later, still unable to accept what had gone down, I went back to the city jail, up to the sixth floor to visit Catarino's partner in the deal-gone-bad.

I didn't know Pablo Damian, the vato on the other side of the glass, I'd never seen him before. The little mustache on his fat face looked smashed by a truck. Bruises still showed from the beating, lots of purple around the bloodshot eyes and a red lump on the jaw.

Damian was facing hard time, so I think he told the truth—why bother lying when you're up for twenty years? This is his story: He and Catarino were scoring a kilo of Mexican tar in Lucky Alley to resell the same day. An easy hundred-percent profit, Damian said. I just listened. They came up to a white car where the connection, a Mexican, waited with a paddy guy. Cat, holding the money, leaned into the car to check out the goods and found a gun pointed at him. "Oh no," Cat said, stepping back from the window. Then the two guys jumped out, guns drawn, no warning, no badges, nothing. While the paddy narc pistol-whipped Damian, Cat scuffled with the Mexican, thinking it was a rip-off. Cat was wrestled to the ground, then—the Mexican narco blasted him point-blank in the forehead. And that was that.

What about the money Cat had on him? I asked. Only about three hundred dollars appeared as evidence in the report. Narcos kept it, never turned it in, he said. I don't know why I asked if Cat had ever mentioned the York Theatre. Chale—not to me, Damian said. That's all I needed to know. I took the elevator down. By the time I reached the bottom floor I felt worse than a piece of liver thrown to dogs, and I just didn't believe anymore in a lot of things.

＋

My life sunk like a U-boat after that. Once Luz got over her initial rage she pretended that nothing was the matter. When she'd moved in, Luz owned a pair of seventy-dollar, spike-heeled shoes, red ones, would wear them when we made love, and she looked like one of those Helmut Newton models, all legs. But now little things, like stashing her red shoes in the back of the closet, told me she was seething inside.

But the worst was yet to come.

Weeks later Luz volunteered as an usher for the San Francisco Film Festival, where she met this Brazilian filmmaker. She hired on as camera for a local documentary he was shooting, but wound up sleeping with him. I came home one day and her cameras were gone—that's all she took—what could I do? She left me a note on the refrigerator telling me she'd moved in with a girlfriend at Project Artaud, the lofts on Florida Street. And not to bother her. Or try to call.

I slipped into darkness, days without a shred of light, and nights filled with bad dreams, ugly as B movie special effects. I couldn't make sense of my emotions. I'd take Luz's clothes and throw them all over the studio, her dresses and bras, angry at the memories these articles brought me. Then I'd neatly hang them in the closet in case she came back. Or I'd crank her editing machine, viewing the negatives she'd shot of me at the Ribeltad, but all I saw were reverse images, dark where it should have been light. And one peek at her red shoes, those spike heels that I kept under our once-happy bed, and I'd walk around torn up for days. At least she wasn't wearing them for the Brazilian.

After the Brazilian left, we ran into each other one night at the Roxie, a showing of *La Hora de los Hornos*. We went for coffee afterwards, and she confessed the Brazilian affair was just revenge for my betraying her. Betraying her how? I asked. By lying to her about the York deal, she said. Too late I remembered her definition of a lie—not telling is also a lie. Well, it's kinda like a half-truth, sort of, and over a half-truth I had destroyed our thing, and now it was impossible to splice us back together like we had been before.

As we finished our coffee she asked when would be a good time to get the rest of her things.

And I said there would never be a good time, but she could come next Saturday.

◆

I still see Luz. Once in a while we get together, sometimes we even make love, punish each other for our sins. I know she doesn't feel the same about me—she gave her sexy shoes to a drag queen at Ésta Noche—and her eyes tend to focus on my scar when we're talking. She keeps saying we're so different because we're from opposite ends of the hemisphere. But I think it's more than two tropic zones that separate us. You make peace with yourself, but there's some wounds that run the length of the continent.

I hadn't thought about Catarino and Lucky Alley in a long time. Soon after all this happened I moved out of Lucky Alley. I went by myself and rented that place above Tede Wong's laundry with some money Toño lent me. I still have hope, still keep the living room cleared of furniture in case Luz decides to move in her editing table.

Usually I take my bus on Potrero. Today, for some reason, I walked down 24th Street to Mission and passed by the York Theatre all boarded up and still dying for affection. This set me thinking how hard I worked to get something going, and yet the results were just the opposite. When I came to Lucky Alley, with its weeds sprouting through cracks in the asphalt, clouds of green flies buzzing over mounds of garbage—I remembered Catarino. I wish I could forgive him, wish I could believe in friendship, honor, and law, but I can't. True, Cat paid the ultimate price—but he also gave me his word with no intention of keeping it. In the barrio a man has only his word and his huevos, but if his word is no good, his balls don't mean a thing.

◆

Sometimes, at four, five in the morning, when I've crawled in from the *jale* and the bedroom walls are striped with shadows cast by the Venetian blinds, I'm too wound up to sleep, so I sit in the empty living room, listening to the buses rumbling below my window and the occasional woosh of a car going by—the only sounds in the city— then the welt from that old scar starts pounding on my forehead like an urgent message, and I think maybe I should have followed up with Brody anyway, tried raising more cash, perhaps I quit too soon. Then I figure—hell, the theater's still available, no reason why I can't do it, right? And just before I doze off, a cozy feeling comes over me and everything seems possible, like the world will spin my way, like when Luz used to kiss me before we fell asleep. But the next morning, in the cruel unforgiving light of day, those dreams burn off like fog.

Today when I passed by Lucky Alley and started think- ing about Catarino and how different my life is now with- out Luz, who seems to be in a movie of her own, her resentment all in technicolor, and how that two-thousand dollars I took from our savings is still a bone of conten- tion—when am I going to pay her back, not to mention the unpaid loan that burned my credit forever, I knew in my heart I would never open the York Theatre. It's all just theory now.

I kept walking to Mission Street, putting Lucky Alley behind me. I don't drive anymore, not since I wrecked the Triumph I was telling you about. I don't drink much either, ever since Luz left me. I don't want to fall into borracheras, they'd only make me miss her more. But that's the worst part of my job, the stink of spilled booze and urine. I should look for something else, but for now I work the plank in a downtown bar, the night run, six days a week till two in the morning doesn't leave much time for the movies.

But I'm not complaining. I wouldn't trade the time I had with Luz for an Oscar. But it's important to move on, even if it's a half step at a time. Next year, if things work out, I want to pay Luz what I owe her so she can finish school and get her degree. Finally. Then maybe she can get out of Channel Five and into something she really loves. She's never stopped dreaming of making films, you know, and it would be a shame to waste her talent. What she doesn't understand is that I threw the dice for both of us. It's true I lost, but my intentions were good. Even after everything that's happened between us, I can't stop loving her, especially now when there is no art or glory in our lives. Sometimes I mention, you know, us trying again, but then Luz falls into those stay-away moods, and I know she's brooding about my betrayal. That's when I feel like someone's dubbed my words into Croatian, or Cyrillic, like I'm in a Russian movie with all the subtitles missing.

When I get to Mission Street, the 14 Mission bus is pulling to the curb and I'm pushed forward by the crowd. I'm in the middle of a mob of high schoolers with their starter jackets, their baseball caps turned backwards. They're all laughing, shouting, shoving, but I clear some way so this little old lady, looks like your abuela in Mexico, can get on with her two hand-held bags. I mean, big deal.

I move to the back of the bus and I'm looking out the graffiti-tagged windows as we go by the New Mission Theater where big red letters on the marquee announce *Corrupción Encadenada* starring Hugo Stiglitz and Patricia Santos, "La Tumbahombres." To me, all these youngsters on the bus are oblivious to the real world. Life to them is a Saturday night flick, something starring themselves, and they're the hero in a fancy car who gets the girl; or they're scheming of doing an ingrata number, cold-hearted, yet they want jewels, a new house, and the leading man, anyway. They're dreaming. Life isn't a movie with El Santo waiting in the wings to rescue you. It doesn't have a script and bright lights and your name in fancy letters. But you can't blame them, you believe what you want to believe. Who wants to hear there's betrayal around every corner, that honor and friendship are lies, that somewhere, someplace, someone's got your name on their knife. But believe me, I know. So watch yourself in Lucky Alley, *carnal*.

# A Lesson in Merengue

The origins of merengue are unknown, though some sources claim that barefooted African slaves chained together at the ankles created the merengue. This restricted movement remains its basic step, an arrogant, sensuous, shuffle to and from the cane fields, dancing to flame the memory of freedom. Other sources claim the merengue was born in 1844 at the battle of Talanquera where Dominican forces defeated an invading Haitian army. These sources claim the merengue step replicates the movement of a wounded soldier.

What is known is that the colonial authorities, scandalized by the sensuality of the dance, forced the merengue underground, where it flourished in the shadows of bateys and sugar centrals, surviving as a thorn in the side of the light-skinned Creole oligarchy. In 1849, in nearby Puerto Rico, General Pezuela even imposed a heavy penalty on the scandalous dance: a fine of fifty pesos for allowing merengue in your house, and ten days in jail for anyone caught dancing it.

In more recent times, the Dominican dictator, Rafael Trujillo, once banned all merengue dancing from the island to prevent a revolution. But people danced anyway, hiding in the hills, waiting for sundown to merengue accompanied by the raspy notes of a country accordion, clapping two sugar cane stalks to keep the beat. When the dictator fell, joyous Dominicans rushed to the Plaza Central and danced merengue out in the open, happy tears mixing with their wild hip rips.

Papá Merengue lives in La Mission too. His main temple is a converted storefront on 17th Street painted blue and white. Every Monday night this becomes the scene of the best merengue lessons in town, taught by the inimitable Agapito Manglar, Dominican dance maestro, whose cool and casual style is charm itself. Step inside and you can hear what the Maestro's saying to his new students:

"Bienvenidos to Monday night at Taller Quisqueya. I take it you're all here to learn merengue, is that correcto? Qué bien. But first let me say this: Merengue cannot be taught like English—like guan, too, tree. No, it's not like that. You have to feel merengue in your bones, in your hips, even your little toes. It's like Papá Merengue that viejito with the slim-hips has to enter your bones and shake your pelvis, and my job is to help him find the address under your dress. You follow me—follow me—get it? So why aren't you laughing?

"You there, Luzma, atención. When you merengue, you want to feel double-jointed, light as a parrot feather, like an orchid floating downstream. With merengue all your problemitas will disappear, your relatives will move out of your living room, the INS will stop harrassing you, and you'll never have to visit that gym down the street. If you're overweight, or maybe had twins like Gina, here, merengue is the best aerobic workout in town. Cheaper too. But if you suffer from padrejón, apretado, cortao, bilirubina, frenesí, resfriado, or any kind of poor health, don't even think about merengue. Your refund is waiting at the door.

"So let's get started—I want all you chicas to grab a partner. Whoever's near you will do. Let's not be choosy girls. That one's fine. We'll start with the merengue pambichao.

"Primero. Loosen up, roll your shoulders, you want to get a nice meneo going like you're stirring chocolate with your hips. Now chicos, slip your right hand around her waist, keeping your left hand at face level. You over there, don't squeeze her like a papaya, guide her with just a little pressure on her waist. Así. Delicado.

"Luzma, honey, hold that man tight, tighter! Ay! He won't bite. In merengue pambichao you dance together stuck like rice—pretend you're shining his belt buckle chica, that's it. Now twist your hips to the right, now to the left. Now—dip your left knee (chicos their right) almost to the floor, come back up. Try it a couple of times till you get the hang of it. Nothing to it, qué no?

"Good. Good. Keep your back straight, Toño, now shuffle to your left, 1, 2, 1, 2, así, nice and suave. Complete the turn and repeat.

"Let me say this to La Betsy over there—heels *will* curve your spine like a flamingo's neck but they'll accent your hip movement and push your flat culito out like a native Caribeña. So tomorrow you'll suffer with a backache from here to Panama, who ever said merengue was painless? If your spine does slip out, Ave María, let's pray not, I recommend Dr. Buenoshuesos, a Latino chiropractor familiar with the heartbreak of merengue.

"Any questions? No? So let's proceed to the next step.

"Ahora—glide across the floor swaying your hips—así, menea para aquí, menea para alla. Repeat. A little faster, Toño, you're not driving a bus, you're dancing merengue.

"OK. Stop. You ready to hear some merengue music? Sí? The typical merengue conjunto comes with accordion, güiro, tambora, and saxophone. A good merenguero follows the beat of the tambora, so listen to this tape of Juan Luis Guerra. Yes. It is fast. But a live band is going to be even faster, the sax jaleo raining a cyclone of notes that's going to drench you in sweat. You'll be dancing so rapido that you'll scream for the fire engines to come put out your shoes. Ave María.

"Now let's try it with the music. Partners ready? Gina? Toño? Uno-dos-ha bailar!

"No, no, no—stop! Oh, you'll need to go mucho mas faster, mi vida. Proper merengue speed is four beats per second. If you can't reach merengue speed, no problemita, but try for at least half-speed, or else the other couples dancing on the floor will stomp you into guava paste.

"You see—compared to the merengue, the cha-cha-cha is a 17th century minuet, and the poor danzón strictly for senile senior citizens. And salsa and cumbia—forget it. They can't shake a güiro to merengue. Of all the Latin dances, the merengue (a pause for dramatic effect) is the King and Queen, the Ace in the deck, the diamond in the tiara, etcetera, etcetera. You get my drift, qué no? So it is our gran placer at the Taller Quisqueya to help you discover the merengue spirit that lives in your hips. After tonight you will feel loco-loca with the music, then you'll be ready to add the trimmings, those fancy moves.

"Pablo, you look adventurous, try spinning your partner like a gyroscope. This way. And Betsy, when you spin, keep your arms up and focus on a fixed object—the bartender who hasn't moved in thirty minutes will do—so you won't get dizzy and toss up that burrito de tofu en salsa roja you had for lunch. Por favor! A warning: Do not, repeat, do not lock fingers with your partner when you spin. I'm sure you've all heard the sad story of Lola Delicias, who broke two fingers while dancing with our ex-instructor Mambo Lopez?

"For the chicos—here's some advice. A little wax on the soles of your shoes never hurt a good merenguero, sabes? A double-breasted suit with a magenta hanky neatly folded in the breast pocket is what the very stylish wear. You get extra points for a tie with flan-colored orchids. Forget the Panama hat, it will fly off your head when you merengue.

"And for you chicas—the Latina spitfire look. Your eyes should sparkle like stars, your lips red as hibiscus, and frizz your hair out to here like a woman chewing on a live wire. A ton of bracelets and gold hoop earrings big as oranges. And tuck that culito into a spandex skirt to accent your curves. Ay, Ave María, I'm not going to tell you how short to wear your skirt. But it should cover at least to here—so if your partner tugs it up, you won't reveal your red thong chonis. Laugh—laugh why don't you. Por favor!

"Chicas, this one is for you: While doing the merengue, think of the fun you have washing beans, or think of your last boyfriend, the Hispanic Republican stockbroker, the one who put you to sleep in the middle of love aerobics. The point is to give the impression that the hottest merengue is too cool for you. Never, ever smile during a merengue, you will come off like the worst turista. If you do smile, do it like a diva, like a true Latina. Arrogant as sin, your nose aimed at the spotlight. Comprendes?

"Now I'm going to offer some free advice like they do on the show de Cristina. When the music hits a frenzy, shimmy as fast as you can without suffering a heart attack or dropping like a coconut from a palmera. A neat trick in merengue is to shake your hips at the speed of sound while keeping your shoulders perfectly squared, like they were nailed to the air.

"And remember—merengue demands style, rhythm, mucho attitude, and a bottle of Ron Barcelo. So now that we've been introduced, who's ready to sign up for our ten-week merengue lessons? Gina? Toño? All of you? Qué chévere.

"But one last thing—before your first lesson, por favorcito, sign this form on the dotted line:

## DISCLAIMER

The management of Taller Quisqueya is not responsible for acts of civil disobedience, spiritual insurrections, or unplanned births that may result from this dancemania. Merengue at your own risk. (A warning: A woman in San Pedro de Macoris claims she was im- pregnated under a full moon by dancing a very hot merengue with a very cool cocolo.) If the merengue is outlawed only outlaws will merengue, our classes will be cancelled, and of course, your money cannot be refunded. So please merengue responsibly.

—Agapito Manglar, owner-manager-instructor,
Taller Quisqueya

So we end this story in the typical Dominican way:

*Y así, colorín, colorao éste cuento se ha acabao.*

# A Toda Máquina

She was hanging around the parking lot at an AM/PM in Sacramento, a little Chicanita with tight jeans tucked into lizard-skin cowboy boots and a small suitcase held together with duct tape. Her sunglasses sparkled with rhinestones giving her a glitzy look that didn't fit in around here, among the trash and homeless pushing shopping carts. This was the rough part of Sacra, where desperate women turned tricks in cars under the shadow of the State Building. She wasn't really hitchhiking me entiendes, but she didn't exactly need a sign that said here was a huiza ready to split Dodge.

I'd nearly finished pumping the fifteen gallons of Supreme when she came up behind me and said, "Can I ride with you to the freeway?" Her voice had something about it that made my stomach tighten up a notch.

I turned around real slow like and there she was in the shimmering heat of the parking lot, suitcase at her feet, hands on her hips, and jeans that looked like she'd taken a brush and painted them on, being careful to detail the seams and pockets. I didn't know if she carried good luck or bad, but I should've guessed. Lizard-skin cowboy boots. Rhinestone sunglasses. A wild bush of hair framing her oval face. I've always been a chump for women, so I said, "Órale, hop in."

Without another word she threw her suitcase in the

back seat and slid in front, against the window, away from me, a coil of plastic bracelets bunched up on her left wrist. I'd been a long time in the country without female company except for Sage Pumo, a Hoopa Indian, wide as a bear, so this little smoke of a woman had most if not all my attention.

I floored the Camaro and shot out of the parking lot. "So what's your name?" she asked. I told her mine and she told me hers—Adelita Guerra. "Nice to meet you," she said. "It's always good to make new friends." She offered her hand, and I shook it. It was a worker's hand, rough and stained from picking walnuts, maybe yesterday. She dug into her front pockets for a frayed pack of Juicy Fruit and offered me one. "Naw. Go ahead," I said. I didn't tell her I hate gum. She chewed, smacking her lips, happy as a kid on a school trip. I had Los Lobos playing on the tape deck, "La Pistola y El Corazón," music that makes you crave a nice cold one. It'd been years since I'd drunk a beer, but you never forget.

When we came to the freeway on-ramp she sat up, "This doesn't look good. Can I ride to the next town?" I glanced at her from the corner of my eye and that tightness in my stomach just got tighter. I couldn't exactly kick her out in the middle of nowhere so I hit the on-ramp with a thump and revved the Camaro out, angry at what I'd gotten myself into.

I kept my mouth shut and my eyes on the road, not wanting to look at her. Still, I could sense her gauging me, like a good hustler on the prowl. On my way to Sacra I'd seen a head-on collision by Redding, two cars twisted into pretzels with no survivors, and that's what I was thinking about a few minutes later when she asked, "Pues, where we going?"

I checked the rear-view mirror for Highway Patrol and ignored her question. Adelita shrugged as if she didn't care, and tapped her boots, grooving to the music. It took a few miles before I settled in to enjoy the big monster working under the hood of my cherry-red Camaro Z-28 that made the white stripes of the road zip by in a blur. A string of red-and-black magic beads swayed from my rear-view mirror, keeping time. Then she started drumming her fingers on the dashboard, like she was playing a piano or something, and I had to sit up and pay attention. She held her head up, like a prize filly, with arrogance and confidence. That's what first pulled me to her, made me question myself. I moved into the fast lane to get clear of an eighteen-wheeler that was hogging the road, but I had no real hurry to get anywhere. I tugged at my goatee and pondered her question. Where are *we* going? *We?* I hadn't thought about us as *we*. More like—her there, and me here. ¿Qué no? I lived happy outside of Weaverville, along a desolate stretch of gravel road at the edge of the Trinity Wilderness, a free man, just me and my music. My nearest neighbor, Sage Pumo, occupied a cabin several miles down Highway 299. At night, I had a clear view of the stars in the California sky. So I didn't need complications, and I had enough grief since my dog Reagan got squashed by a logging truck.

I looked her in the eye, "I'm headed south."

"Then I'll ride with you. I'm going to Vegas."

I took a closer look at her. "Why's that?"

"I'm a singer. I sing rancheras, huapangos, boleros. I also play the accordion. I'm going to be a star."

"There's a lot of talent in Vegas. Lots."

She frowned for just a second, like that thought had never crossed her mind.

"But I'm good, I'm real good. When I sing I feel it all inside me. In here." And she jabbed a thumb at her heart.

Man, some people are real naive. I didn't want to discourage her with tales of good girls gone bad selling themselves for a dime of meth so I flipped the tape to the other side.

We were crossing the heart of the San Joaquin Valley, miles of tomatoes and strawberries separated by irrigation ditches, and crop dusters flying low, spraying a fine pesticide mist over the perfectly laid out furrows. Two thin vapor trails, almost faded, crossed in the eggshell blue of the sky. The sun was slanting down behind us, setting the mountains on fire. Adelita removed her sunglasses and laid them on the dashboard. She squinted at the mean farm fields, and the corner of her eyes crinkled up where the first crow's-feet were beginning to take a grip. She crossed one knee over the other, drummed her fingers some more on the armrest, and hummed a tune I couldn't make out. I didn't want to stare at her, but she was kinda pretty in a country sort of way. In her late twenties, I guessed. Don't get me wrong, Adelita seemed game, like she'd been around the block a couple of dozen times. Her mouth had that hard edge women get after twenty-five when they figure out life's not going to treat them right.

But I wanted some details. "So where you from?"

She tossed her head back over one shoulder. "From there."

"Sacramento?"

"Colusa."

Colusa, land of dust and walnuts. I could see why she'd want to leave. "How'd you get to Sacra?"

She answered with a throaty, wicked laugh that stood the hairs on my arm at attention.

I took a wild guess. "You running away?"

"You could say that."

"A bad relationship?"

"Sort of."

"What? Husband?"

"Are you loco? No husband."

"You have family? Kids?"

"You sure ask a lot of questions."

"Maybe you should go back."

"Never."

"The kids'll be worried about you. I can always turn around."

"Try it and I'll jump out right here. I'll never let a man tell me what to do. Ever. I'm through with that."

I could tell she was serious. And it really wasn't my business. We passed Santa Nella and I had the Camaro doing eighty and thinking that driving alone ain't so bad. I checked the fuel gauge and figured out when I would need to make another pit stop. Up ahead, a black, ominous cloud funneled out of the middle divider, something was burning. I eased off a notch on the gas.

I noticed she was staring at my tats.

I had the Virgen of Guadalupe emblazoned in India ink on my right forearm. Two chubby angels beneath her feet unfurled a banner that said Perdoname Virgencita. On each knuckle of my right hand was tattooed a letter. My other forearm had a blue heart, and inside the heart Norma/Por Vida. I was sixteen when I did that one. I even had a little Native American glyph on my shoulder for Sage.

Adelita was eyeballing the Virgen, so I said, "You want to touch? Go ahead."

She scooted closer to me and touched the Virgen de Guadalupe. Her fingernails were like needles puncturing my skin. She left her hand on my arm a second longer than necessary, as if feeling my strength.

"Ever seen tats like these?" I said.

"Not really. Where'd you get them?"

I shrugged. "Tough tattoos. Long, sad stories."

"You don't want to tell me, do you? What's the matter, don't you trust me?"

"It's not a question of trust."

"What is it then? You afraid I'll tell the *National Enquirer*?"

Crazy woman. I don't know why I said, "You'd look real fine with one."

She shot a look at me that burned right through my skull.

"Where would you put it?"

That surprised me. Where would *I* put it? Where would I tattoo her for life? I pressed my thumbnail just under her blouse into her shoulder, leaving a red mark like a half moon. The air around that part of the valley must have been highly charged with electric particles because touching her hit me like a live wire. A pure jolt of energy. I would not lie, *carnal*. At the same time, I saw the object on the middle divider was a semi rig that had jackknifed, the steel cab all mangled, charred, and smoking like a plane wreck. A fire crew hosed the wreckage with streams of water, but it was too late. No man could have survived that accident. We passed by it in a flash.

Adelita scooted back to her seat and I mentally rehearsed the business I had in El Ley. Under a false compartment in the trunk were forty Ziploc bags of red-haired sinsemilla. This stash belonged to Sage, her whole harvest. Her first husband had left her seven hundred acres of prime mountain real estate complete with underground springs, her second husband had left her a tractor. I was just her neighbor and a hired hand, but already I felt like husband number three. I helped plant the seedlings during the spring and watered them in summer, running a PCV pipe from the underground source to the budding plants. Sage held the main percentage, and I usually made enough to keep in buds during the winter months and, if I was lucky, to survive till the next harvest. This year, though, I had offered to unload the crop with my main man in Pico Rivera. Tyrannus Mex was a boxcar of meanness, the main connect in East Los, and he paid cash on the line. So I was making the run with ten pounds of the highest grade herb in the world. Real triple-A stuff. Sage and I were looking at maybe fifty grand in pure profits, just like the big boys running paper scams. My percentage would be enough to live in style for a whole year.

But working up close in the mountains has a way of stripping you down to bare emotions. After toiling in the herb garden I would relax with Sage in the sweat lodge where I had a chance to consider her ample, hairless body and her sizable breasts under braided black hair. One of her nipples pointed up and the other pointed down, and that just increased my curiosity. During those late summer months a female bear had taken to showing up every morning around my cabin, and when the bear started looking good I feared for my sanity. So instead I squeezed my skinny hips between Sage's broad thighs and she rubbed us both to warmth and human comfort.

The night before my trip, Sage and I were snuggled under her Pendleton blanket. Suddenly she sat up. "Maybe you'd better not make this trip. I had a dream last night about you, and your luck's about to run out." "Naw," I said to Sage, "I don't believe in dreams." Then we humped like bears in the woods, with lots of growls and thrusts and groans and moans, but not much passion. Sleeping with Sage Pumo wasn't exactly love, but it was convenient.

I did have other business in El Ley, and the thought of it kept me quiet for miles. El Ley had stopped being my town a long time ago. I was going back to bury my only brother, a half brother really. Even though he was the product of my father's affairs, and we never lived in the same house, we spent a lot of time together as teenagers. We have a saying in the barrio that fit the two of us—Blood is thicker than mud. But he'd been on the streets a while, and I'd lost touch with him. Ten years maybe without hearing from him, then the yellow envelope from the V.A. office with the cold notice. He'd either been robbed or beaten, or both, with nothing in his pockets but thirty-four cents when they found him drowned in the El Ley River. The El Ley River that's about three inches deep. I wondered if they would bury him with the box full of medals he'd brought back from Vietnam. He'd been an honor student in high school—who would have guessed this would be his end? But it was. And the anger of it kept me burning, kept me awake many nights. I was going back because it was the right thing, but I wanted to leave quick and clean before the jaws of El Ley clamped down on me again.

Adelita pressed her knees together and withdrew into her own world. I scraped all thoughts about her out of my mind and drove on. We were by Kettleman City, the road like an arrow aimed at nothing, the sky big as a canvas, with two small puff clouds blowing across the blueness like tumbleweeds. The only signs on the road warned— Patrolled by aircraft. This empty land could make anyone a desperado.

"I'm taking this exit." I said. "You decide what you want to do."

She sat up, looking at me as if I'd insulted her, then she

turned away and looked out the window, like there was something to see, the Grand Canyon perhaps.

After parking, I went to the head and took a long leak, taking my time to shake my thing dry, hoping that maybe Adelita would be gone by the time I got back. But when I stepped out there, she was still scrunched down in the car. So I bought a pack of sunflower seeds in the Quick Stop and kept my eyes on her just in case she'd step out to stretch her legs or use the head. But she wasn't taking any chances. I felt sorry for her and brought her a soda when I came back.

"I guess that means you want to ride," I said.

"That's right," she said.

If women are a puzzle, this one had a thousand mismatched pieces. I pulled back onto the freeway and tried the radio for a while, but picked up nothing but static and a country preacher begging donations and spewing hate and prejudice. Just what this country needs. So I snapped it off. Adelita was chewing on a hangnail, not looking at the road.

Finally I said, "So what songs you know?"

She looked at me like a puppy that wants to please. "You want me to sing?"

"No. I want you to tap dance backwards."

She put one hand over her mouth to hide her smile. Then she sang, bajito at first, a little unsure of herself, one of those classic boleros from long ago, "Perfidia," a song of passion, heartache, and betrayal. Linda Ronstadt had nothing to worry about. Not yet anyway. Adelita went off-key on the high notes, and she forgot every other line and just kinda scatted her way through the lyrics. But her voice and phrasing simmered with raw emotion that moved even a cold-hearted vato like me. With a few lessons, who knows how far she'd go?

Then she did something I wish she hadn't done. She hummed a few bars of "Historia de un Amor" and I remembered everything I wanted to forget. Of all the songs in the world "Historia de un Amor" held bitter memories of three summers I wasted in Soledad Prison, lifting weights, playing dominos, killing some slow time. Another pinto, Shorty from Visalia, a tattoo artist with a disfigured face, did my tats. He plucked a thread from a blanket, tied three needles to a popsicle stick, then dipped the jail-house invention in a bottle of India ink. He outlined the Virgen first, a jab at a time, then filled in the details, the rays shooting out behind her, the hands folded in prayer, the two angels. It was my idea to add the banner and the words. Working from a photograph, Shorty made the Virgen look like Reina Sarmiento, my outside woman. Later, he did the moon and the stars at her feet. It took him six months to finish. This was late at night work, another pinto keeping a lookout for the bulls, while Shorty worked the needles, and each jab stung like a betrayal or a false kiss. At lock-down time, with the cell block quiet, I spent each night in my bunk tracing the cracks on the grey ceiling, knowing my friends were living their lives, having kids, going to parties, and I was doing time, eating off metal plates, walking the yard, watching my back, and going to sleep rubbing my cock to those train whistles blowing lonesome as coyotes, wondering if anyone remembered me on the outside. And her singing that one song brought it all back, indelible as any tattoo.

After Adelita finished she was silent for a moment, like she was waiting for the applause. I was lost in my own memories.

"What do you think?" she asked.

"You're sad. But you have talent."

She cracked a smile and I noticed she had one black tooth near the back of her mouth. "The minute I saw you, I could tell you were the man for me."

Let me tell you, *carnal*, sometimes a man gets tempted to throw everything away for a woman. Like there's one of those Oaxacan carnival devils on your shoulder, the ones with the red horns, giving you bad advice. Just pushing you to do something stupid. A man has to be on guard for these moments. And it looked like one of these moments was upon me. I took a closer look at her. She wasn't much you could hold on to, thin as a fence post really, and that Colusa soil still dirtied her nails. But I had a powerful urge to bury my face in that wild hair of hers and smell it. I wanted to feel what it was like to squeeze her in my arms and wake up in the morning with her dark face next to mine. And I could feel myself sinking into her temptation like I was waist deep in quicksand.

I'd stayed away from temptation for years. Especially Chicanitas, my only heavy vice, those brown girls. I'd been through the bad hurt before. Real bad. Back in the days with Reina Sarmiento. My one true love. My always and forever babe. Her name in blue letters on the knuckles of my right hand. I ruined my life for her, lost three years in Soledad, taking the rap when we were busted holding two kilos of some potent Jamaican ganja. I threw a beer can at the cops when they busted the door down and got an assault tacked on the possessions charge. That meant a felony, some extra time. And when I came out, what did Reina have waiting for me? I had a stash of nearly ten grand before the take down, and she couldn't tell me where the money was. Down her arm and up her nose. I loved that woman so much, had kissed every nook and cranny of her body, had dipped my tongue between her legs and over her breasts, now I wouldn't kick her in the ass if she bent over. So you see? That's why I don't believe in love.

After the pinta I had gone north to get as far as I could. To get as far from the grief and drugs and booze of East Los as probation would allow. Now my colors were neither red nor blue, I was neither norteño nor sureño. This was my first trip back in ten years, and I was tense. I meant to make the deal with T-Mex, sign the forms for my brother's funeral, and be out within twenty-four hours. And never go back.

Adelita pulled down the sun visor, then, looking in the mirror, rolled her hair up and knotted it in a bun. A small curl slipped out of the knot and down her nape and that just drove me crazy. Right there I would have sold my soul to hang like that curl and kiss the back of her neck. She reached into the back seat and hauled her suitcase up front, ripped the tape off, and I could see all she had in there was a beat-up accordion and a pint of peach brandy. The real sweet stuff. She shoved the bottle at me.

"Have a drink with me, cowboy."

I licked the dust from my lips. "No thanks."

I fished in the ashtray for the joint I'd been hitting on the night before with Sage. Up to this minute I had forgotten about her premonition. Now here I was with a woman who was a dream chaser.

I fired up the roach with the car lighter, sucked in a little jet stream of smoke, and held my breath like a blowfish. Then I blew a rush of purple smoke that clouded the Camaro. I'd been sober for years, just smoked a little—once a vato loco, always a vato loco, and the last thing I wanted was to start drinking. Booze was poison to me; I had too much Indian blood, that's what Sage told me. But Adelita tipped the bottle to her lips, and a thin line of brandy trickled down her mouth. I noticed her mouth, wide with full lips, the kind I like. She wiped her mouth with the palm of her hand.

I was holding the roach with my fingernails. "Care for a hit?"

"No. It's bad for my voice."

Once the herb came on, the landscape stretched out, the seconds floated by, and the miles seemed further apart though I kept a steady eighty. A bug went Splat! on the windshield, leaving a dribble of yellow liquid. I could feel the bug's pain, its surprise at suddenly flying into something solid when it thought the sky was clear. Splat! There went another one. I was too sensitive to be in the fast lane so I moved over to the middle lane and slowed to seventy. And I thought of Shorty doing hard time in Soledad. A woman he loved had poured scalding water on him while he slept, leaving half his face melted like wax. But he survived the county hospital doctors. Months later, he ran into his ex-wife and her new vato, in the Reno Club in Sacra. Shorty didn't care about her anymore, but a fight started anyway and he stabbed the vato with a five-inch blade, right in the neck. So now one man was paralyzed and another in prison, and the woman who'd caused it all flew off free as a golondrina. Pobre Shorty. He should have walked away from her when he had the chance. Poor stupid Shorty. I learned in the joint there's nothing more dangerous than loving a woman the way Shorty had loved, blind as a worm, the way I had loved Reina Sarmiento. The woman didn't exist that was worth your life. And I intended never to love a woman, any woman, that bad, again. But that was the only way I knew how. And faking it with Sage was the coward's way out.

Adelita turned quiet too, she hunched in her corner of the front seat, her knees crossed and didn't sing anymore, just sipped her brandy through tight lips. Every now and then she'd take a quick glance at me then look away. The only sound came from my Camaro ripping off the miles. After a while she turned to me, with just a hint of pleading in that voice I would have followed anywhere.

"I need a ride to Vegas," she said. "You want to take me,

be with me when I make it?"

I couldn't believe it. Why did I always find the crazy ones? The ones even the devil didn't want. "It doesn't work that way," I said. "You can't just take two people from the middle of nowhere and mix them."

She glared at me, eyes all fired up with anger. "Why not? Or do you want that whole game-playing first? Tú sabes, the sweet-talking and the playing around like you don't know what you're after. I'm through with that. Either you come with me or you don't. I'm not asking you again." She pinned me down with those arrowhead eyes of hers.

I stuffed the last handful of sunflower seeds in my mouth and crushed them viciously. Hell, I knew I could get along with her, I could tell, but Virgen María, what was she like day after day? Passion is fleeting—I knew that much. One morning you wake up and they want to sit on your face and you just can't handle it that early, even with the most beautiful woman, so that kills the romance right there. And she was tough, the type that would get back at you while you slept. I could see that. Maybe she poisoned her ex-old man, and that's what she was running from. Or maybe her ex was getting ready to come after her. Maybe there was no ex, maybe it was a husband. So there was that to worry about. She didn't seem too concerned about her kids, either. And I didn't need troubles. I especially didn't need her troubles.

Just to test her I said, "You maybe have money to get there? You know the old saying, Gas, Grass, or *Ass*."

"I'll pay you somehow."

I turned my eyes back to the road. "Chale," I said, "I have business in El Ley."

That hurt her. She stared out the window for a while, like there was something to see, but I knew there was nothing out there. Finally she spoke, pleading but not pleading.

"You don't seem like a bad man. That's all I've ever known. Since I was fifteen."

I didn't want to listen to the oldest story in the world.

"A woman needs some kind of protection. Or else bad men will take advantage of her." She tilted the bottle up and took a long swallow. Wiped her mouth with her hand again. "It's not easy raising two kids alone. And no man wants a woman with kids, I don't blame them. But all I've ever wanted to do was sing. I'd sing in the fields, just to ease that pain in my corazón, right here where it hurts all the way through your back. I'd sing under the trees during lunch time, or after work, whenever I could. And people were always saying I should get paid for it and they'd pass the hat. You know what you get paid for picking walnuts?"

"I don't really care," I said.

"Not very fucking much."

She took a deep breath, shook her head, took another drink. Now she really unleashed it on me.

"My last boyfriend, you know, he did some things to me . . . ."

Damn, I wanted to stop the car, get out right there in the middle of nowhere, and show her not all men were animals.

"So I left my two boys with their abuelita. And split."

"I'm glad you did." And I looked at her, sitting sad as a bird on a wire in winter.

"I'm sure you had to," I said.

"But you're different, I can see that. You have corazón, like me." And she took another swig and smiled, looking like a little girl. A little girl on the run, telling stories and nipping her brandy.

The honesty of her confession wrapped around me like tule fog and there was nothing else to say. I thought about a woman like her, alone on the road, making her way with strangers who offered rides. The sort of trouble she could get into—being kinda good-looking, and a little crazy and all. Leaving her kids behind must have hurt some, I guess. And who knows what that boyfriend did to her; she'd probably been chained to the stove, or worse, and this was her only chance, her last chance at life. It was tragic. I mean there was a tragedy waiting to happen, and I didn't want it to happen. I had to admire her taking the risk, getting set one day, packing her things into that patched-up suitcase and slipping out to chase her dream. I just didn't know where I fit in. I'd wasted the first half of my life already, and I sure didn't want to blow the rest over a piece of nearly flat Chicana ass.

Before my life had gone to hell I'd been a guitarist, sat in on some of the first gigs Los Lobos played when they were still a garage band. Five years passed, and then time in the joint, and after I came out I didn't remember what I had started out to be. Didn't give a damn either. Now I only wanted to live my life, die in peace, be buried and forgotten. My dreams had withered in the day-to-day survival. But something about Adelita was rubbing off on me. Just watching her sit there, a hurricane being born, I felt the itch to do things again, to take chances. Live life at full throttle. It was that funny feeling I'd gotten when I'd first seen her.

The green freeway sign read Los Angeles 90 Miles. I'd been driving six hours, I was tired and thirsty, the thin film of dust over the Camaro seemed to cover me too. I turned to her and said in a voice I didn't recognize, "Let me have a sip of that brandy." That was my choice. Had nothing to do with her. I washed some of that cheap stuff down my throat and handed her back the pint. My eyes burned like I was giving up the ghost.

She was measuring me. "I bet I know what you're thinking."

"What's that?" I squinted at the road so she couldn't read my mind.

"You'd like to kiss me."

"It's pretty hard when I'm doing seventy on I-5."

But a kiss is not what I was thinking. I was thinking I had just taken my first drink in ten years and was ready for more. The road to damnation—someone once said—is paved with wine, women, and weed, and I had a full house. I checked the rear-view mirror. The magic red-and-black beads that my shaman friend Maestro Andres had given me hung like a broken piñata, and they seemed to have lost the power to protect me. Adelita slid over next to

me and placed her hot little hand on my thigh. The speed-
ometer went straight up.

With Adelita I knew it was going to be all the way, all
the time, without regrets, double or nothing. I checked her
out sideways and I said, "What about that tattoo?"

Without so much as a blink she reached up and pulled
down a corner of her blouse revealing a sunburned shoulder. The red half moon of my nail mark was still visible on
her skin. Her voice a sultry whisper wicked as a night on
the delta: "I've never been tattooed."

I thought of Reina and Sage and all the other huizas I
carry stitched on my body. But here was a woman willing
to do it for me. Willing to go all the way—*a toda máquina.*

"A heart on fire is what I'm going to put there. Then
we'll be a pair. Por Vida."

She leaned over and blew her hot breath in my ear. My
foot went to the metal and the Camaro took off, as if wanting to fly. Then she pressed a hot kiss on my mouth, her
plastic bracelets clacking in my ear. This is it, I thought, no
going back. I closed one eye and swerved down the middle
of that four-lane highway, knowing there was not another
car on the road, only her and me, our tough tattoos, and
the radials running over those little plastic squares that
separate the lanes, going fuckit, fuckit, fuckit.

# THIS WAR
# CALLED LOVE

A conjunto classic, "Mi Tesoro," will be playing in the background, and candles burning, and yet—you'll have your doubts when she slips the Virgen de Guadalupe around your neck, the gold medallion cold and heavy against your heart. Her name will be Lupita, she'll be a rising conjunto star who sings songs of love and war, and like her namesake Virgen, she'll attract men who believe in miracles. Though you have never worn a medallion or made promises to virgins, Lupita will become your devotion, the central altarpiece of your profane life.

Still, after all, you'll worry about her adoring public— there's Rip in Tucson, and Rasguño in Las Cruces, even a Reata somewhere between El Paso and Nogales. But she'll say the virgencita is for you only, she carried it all through her tour, carried it for weeks thinking of you. And it's meant to seal her love. Then she'll kiss the bright medallion swinging from your neck, and make a promise in the future tense: "I will never leave you. Not ever." Later on, too late to make a difference, you'll wonder about that promise—was it for real or just made up like the lyrics of her songs?

Before each performance she will transform into her persona, Lupita, La Soldadera, the Soldier Woman. Since you've been with her you'll have picked up conjunto, the rustic music of the Southwest—for the urban man you are, it's like picking up cigarettes from the street. It took a while for the acordeón to weave its charm, but now because she plays it you'll adore every note squeezed from that box. Salsa and merengue, your natural-born music, will be tossed aside like the two-tone dancing shoes under your bed.

Every day you'll drag yourself to Double Rock, the lost corner of the City, where homeless men line the streets begging for cigarettes. You'll work with Mexicanos, indocumentados, whose hands are rough as their jokes. They'll raz you when Lupita's songs play on the Mexican station, but it'll make you proud, a real gallo, because your girlfriend doesn't get her hands dirty, because she's a star (even if it's just small time), and they're just envious. So you'll ignore their jibes, and you'll fire up the welding torch, adjust the valves of oxygen/propane till you get a pure blue flame. You'll flip down the plastic face shield and go to work with the acetylene. The life expectancy in your job is ten years. You'll have five left which you'll give to Lupita in the future tense.

When your compadre sees the Lupe medallion, big as the dark rings under your eyes, he'll warn you, "You can't trust conjunto singers, they don't know what they want."

You'll say, "She swore on the Virgen de Guadalupe."

He'll say, "What if she's not a true believer?"

You'll have no answer for that. His left sleeve is pinned to his shoulder, a bitter reminder of another war. You'll swallow hard. All you know is what you feel.

Your compadre will cup his hands to show cojones big as grapefruits. "Agarate de los huevos. Keep your pride. Don't be a pendejo, you're just another one of her cabrones."

You'll picture pride as a bayonet across your balls. You'll care about your huevos but not about false pride.

Late at night, doubts will torment you when street conjuntos wander outside your window, yowling like cats in heat:

> *Si Lupita se fuera con otro*
> *La seguiria por tierra y por mar*

†

When Lupita stays the night in your one room studio, you'll wake before she does and spend the first minutes studying her face, memorizing each dimpled scar and pore on her skin. She'll awake, looking more beautiful than the night before, the sheets around her waist, and her smile like sunrise in the tropics. While you cook breakfast, homemade burritos and Mexican coffee, she'll pull out a pencil and write lyrics she'll say you have inspired. She'll hum a melody and press the ivory buttons of her green-white-red Hohner acordeón to make it sing—forty-six buttons, one for every heart she's broken. Her voice will fill your sleepy head, you'll ignore the rumors about broken hearts and abandoned men—instead you'll believe you understand her. You'll tell her you admire that she's strong, powerful, artistic, and brave. It's not about washing the dishes, you'll tell her as you're washing the dishes. And you'll leave it at that.

She'll leave hints about the future. "I have a recurring nightmare of losing my voice, it makes me nervous and high strung. A diva in other words." Or she asks a question you can't answer: "Don't you think woman should be independent?" Or she'll confess: "My ambition is to play New York, sign a giant contract, and have a platinum record." And you'll wonder what's this have to do with you?

Instead you'll kiss her tiny hands, and all her pretty fingers, the ones she writes the lyrics with, and you'll say, "You are my biggest battle of this war called love."

And she'll say, "I'm looking for the one. Just like in music. I find the one, the beat, then I'm in step."

She'll clap the beat for you. 1-2-3. 1-2-3-4.

You'll feel out of place at her concert, hanging around Obrero Hall, a working-class hangout in La Mission, all the men in white cowboy hats, you the only vato in a black one. Then the velvet curtain will rise and she'll step onto center stage, into the sapphire spotlight—red-fringed skirt, rebozo crisscrossed like bandoleers, arms wrapped around her accordion. She'll stomp the beat with her combat boots, toss her head back and rip into her first song. Her voice will flow like biblical honey, she'll sing love is a short fuse, some gasoline and a match, una bomba de contacto. The lyrics will spread over the crowd, flares bursting in air, a battle hymn for her army of adoring fans.

You'll push forward, crowding the stage, wanting her like every man and woman on the sawdusty floor. The men will howl like wolves and make kissing sounds; the women will throw flowers and scream her name. You'll see how she glows in the adoration, how the hall shakes with applause when she smiles, how her ego runs higher than a full-moon tide. You'll find deep meaning in every one of her songs, even the instrumentals. You'll be embarrassed at how much you crave her, like a dervish does his whirling, an Assyrian assassin his hashish. You'll want to pin her like a Purple Heart upon your chest, shameless proof that she has picked you. You'll struggle to conjugate the future tense, something you were never good at in high school: I believe, I shall believe, I will believe.

But doubts will drag you back into the present.

At night when you close your eyes the torch flame will dance in your brain, a fiery apparition. And in the quivering blue fire Lupita will appear with her accordion and her fringed skirt and combat boots. She'll sway like a candle that won't go out. One night you'll dream you're a gray cat that slips into her new bedroom—you'll see everything so clear, the pumpkin-colored walls, the brick-red dado, and iron-framed mirrors. You'll watch her a long time, sleeping in her sheets fluffy as whipped cream. The next night you'll dream her sleeping with another man and you'll wake up with your heart ticking like a bomb.

When the Mexicanos ask about Lupita, you'll just smile and nod, but you won't be kidding anyone with that long face. So you'll turn to the torch for comfort. This is what you'll live for now, the blue flame of redemption, absolution. Twelve-hour days welding is a joy. Sparks from your torch are hotter than the devil's tongue. You'll cauterize your doubts like the steel rods you bend and pound into something they have no idea of being. Metal shavings will get in your hair, under your fingernails, clog your throat, but it won't matter. The clanging of hammers against the anvil will drown out your demons. Your life will resemble a Dostoevsky novel, but with all the happy parts cut out, more like a tableau from hell.

The next time she comes around you'll ask her a few questions, not wanting to be nosy. "Don't be silly, what other men?" she'll say. "I always dedicate a song to you, at all the dances, weddings and quinceañeras I play."

Then she'll hang her accordion on your bedpost, slip her ruffled skirts off and let her hair fall in thick strands over her dark nipples. Hooking one finger around the gold medallion of Guadalupe, she'll draw you to her like she was pulling you by the hair. You've become a captive of this flowery war, a slave to her desire. You'll kiss the nopalito, the cactus tattooed on her hip, press your lips the whole length of her long, long legs, fall on your knees and kiss her boots caked with sawdust and won't even realize what you're giving up.

Perhaps it's the way she looks in your bed, naked, reclining on your worn zarape blanket, or the way she devours you under the zarape, totally, con tantas ganas, and makes you feel she could do this with just one man, you lucky guy. Maybe it's the way she wraps her arms around you till the arrows of the alarm clock pierce your head, or how sometimes you both dream the same dream (and you'll forget your dream of her with other men). Whatever it is, you'll have the medallion swinging from your neck, believing in Lupita with each heartbeat the virgencita rides. You'll even imagine the two of you together, inseparable as a first name and a last typed on a birth certificate. And you'll ignore the voice inside your head that whispers you're crazy, stupid, trading your present for a future promised down the road.

You're compadre will stop coming around because you don't have time for him since Lupita takes it all anyway.

A week before the Cinco de Mayo she'll pack her accordion and her boots for a concert in El Paso. You'll say goodbye like in a Mexican movie, fucking on the sofa, half-dressed and everything. You'll feel the best you've ever felt, solid, secure in her affection. Then you'll find the note from Razor saying he'll meet her at the airport. You'll know this Razor guy, a sharply dress conjunto singer who plays the tololoche, the stand up bass and drives a late-model Continental with big, wide steer horns on the hood. He'll keep a better beat whereas you only kept the fire. The little world you built out of promises will spin in confusion. Her voice will haunt your every waking minute, you'll hear it everywhere, at bus stops, cafés, even the old ladies selling flowers on the streets will sound like her. You'll hear the conjunto band outside your window playing that corrido about a woman who runs off with sailors and soldiers. It won't help your mood any.

You'll spend a week alone on a tremendous borrachera, roaming the trash blown streets of La Mission, lost as Ché in Bolivia. You'll hit the clubs where you won't hear conjunto music, Galia's, the Roccapulco on Mission Street, the Tin-Tan Club. You'll do the bar scene on 16th Street, just another shipwrecked man searching for a port. In shadowy booths you'll rediscover what it's like to kiss women that taste of sour mash and whose names you don't care to know. You'll squeeze offered breasts, hips, thighs. You've heard said that all women are the same, two tits and a pussy, but you'll know different. Lupita was not like other women, una cualquiera. She was the woman you adored right up there with Selena and Salma Hayek. In spite of your best efforts, you'll bump into Lupita's memory in every bar, in every jukebox pleading, "Come back, baby, come back." Her face in every blue neon sign advertising Lone Star Beer.

In the morning you'll wake up on the couch with the sun roasting your brain and you won't recognize your room. When did the cockroaches, sipping tequila from your shot glass, move in? Cigarette burns on your rug? You'll struggle to your feet, and you'll stand there all wobbly and crudo, the gold medallion swaying from your neck like a ten-ton weight.

It will be Cinco de Mayo, the anniversary of a heroic battle between bare-footed Mexicans wielding machetes against French dragoons and zouaves—the cream of European armies—and there will be a message from Lupita on your answering machine. You'll hear her voice say she's been invited to Austin, then Albuquerque. Maybe New York afterwards, her big break at last. She doesn't know when she'll be back, but she'll stay in touch, and ends with, "A girl has to do what's best for herself. You understand, don't you?" You'll play the message fifteen times to make sure you understand it. Her words will be a fuse attached to your heart, burning toward a fiery explosion that blows you to pieces.

You won't believe it but she's gone, el golpe avisa.

It'll be a scorcher, heat buckling the asphalt. The weather will remind you of adobe walls and firing squads and Lupita, *La Soldadera*—those three days you spent together in the cabin and how starry the sky appeared the night you shared blue-green peyote buttons. On the ride back to the City you stopped at Guadalupe Creek, dust remolinos swirling like crazy lovers along the sandy banks. You'll recall her skin, the amber tint that is hers and hers alone. How you loved to press your mouth to that tasty color. Press your body to hers like that night on the sandy banks of the creek, her red-fringed skirt up over her waist, both of you rolling against the current. That memory buried in your flesh was a tough bullet, tough to dig out.

Depressed, you'll turn to your best friend, your only friend, tequila. Bitter as wasted tears. But you'll not cry, not going to cry her love. With furious *ajuas!*, with straight shots of tequila you will forget her al estilo Jalisco. What's more, you'll forget what day of the week it is, forget to shave, brush teeth, change clothes, work. You'll live in shadows where giant vultures of despair gnaw your liver. It'll be the year when blue agave tequila is all the rage,

100% straight, and you'll drink this tequila by the bottle till an aqueous cobalt light soothes and wraps you like her arms once did.

Through all your lonely nights, the Guadalupe medallion will burn on your chest like mustard gas in the trenches of your insomnia. You'll kiss it, pray to it, beg the Virgen for a word from Lupita. One terrible night, in a moment of religious weakness you'll even promise a pilgrimage to the Tepeyac. Promise you'll cross the plaza on your knees if Lupita comes back. But all you'll hear is the wind in the street, and the loneliness will clamp on you, a steel trap on a desperate coyote. You'll learn that's how it ends for the greatest passion of your life, not with a bang but with the long echo of silence.

At this point you'll have no choice but to reinvent all the words for adiós—Good-bye corazón, ciao chula, toddleoo muñeca, al rato ésa, and hasta la vista. Finito Lupita.

Because of her you'll withdraw from the world, ignore the phone, stop going out, sullen as a jailbird. Because of her the stars become broken rubies scattered across a canvas the color of her eyes. You'll wear out each night in blancas borracheras to scour her memory. You'll lose the will to live and go through the whole Humphrey Bogart-Pedro Arméndariz-Agustín Lara number, pound your fist on the table and knock over the bottle. And you'll play those songs, over and over, all her conjunto favorites, "Ambición," "El Muro," "Mi Tesoro," especially "Mi Tesoro," the song she swore by. You'll dance by yourself in your unlit room, bottle of tequila in one hand, cigarette in the other, stumbling over your bare feet. Her words will spin in your head like drunken conversations: "I will never leave you, I will never, I will." You'll feel betrayed by the future tense; no wonder you hate the mañana syndrome. You'll realize you mistook her for a woman of her word. Hecha y derecha. A la brava.

In your vale-verga-don't-give-a-damn mood you'll let things go a la madre, all the way to hell. Just like that. Dishes stacked in the sink and unwashed, cigarette butts all over the floor, mail stuffed in drawers. Dust an inch thick everywhere. Till one morning you'll reach for the records you have played a hundred times and discover the sun has warped them all. Worse than month-old tortillas.

Your compadre will drop by, worried, wanting to know how you've been doing. You'll rub the stubble on your chin, "Like Cuauhtémoc with his feet to the fire." He'll lay a C-note on you, not to worry about paying him back. Then he'll talk about the war in Vietnam, the arm amputated at the shoulder. He still feels his missing arm, it still hurts him, and that was thirty years ago. Now that was a war he'll say. He'll leave shaking his head. "Don't say I didn't warn you 'bout that little girl."

You'll send fifty bones to Roy in Austin, Texas, for some rattlesnake meat he connects from an old Yaqui in the desert. The package will arrive the day you are contemplating the damage a sawed-off shotgun might do to a human head. Yours specifically. It might even come just as you're loading the shotgun. You'll set aside the double-barrel, open the package and stare at the contents: dried, rust-red rattlesnake meat. You'll take a bite, chew slowly. It'll be tough as her heart and taste like buzzard, funky old road-kill buzzard. You'll swallow it anyway. Then before the altar you've set up in your living room, with postcards of Geronimo, Ricardo Flores Magón, Pancho Villa, Ché, and the Santo Señor de Chalma, you'll burn sage and cedar and copal. You'll need fuerza. Lots of it. You will remove the medallion of Guadalupe, and it will make you light-headed, as if you came up too fast from the ocean bottom. You will place the Virgen on your manly altar, hoping it will balance things out. But you've given up on prayer, given up on hope. Only yourself can save you now.

You'll decide to ride this one out cold turkey, sober. Every dawn, while the lights of the city still burn, you'll rise and meditate, then run up on Bernal Heights, training like you were going to a barroom brawl against Mike Tyson. You'll watch your intake of food and pop vitamins like they were cherries. After you do your hundred daily crunches, you'll sip tea and read Sun Tzu and Ché, to help you through this war. From Sun Tzu: "Invincibility depends on one's self." And from Ché: ". . . no battle, combat, or skirmish is to be fought unless it will be won."

Forgetting is an art and you'll be writing the book *Love and the Art of Forgetting*. Chapter One: Once you forget, that's it. No queda nada. Not the sound of her voice, or the black pearls of her eyes.

In Spanish, olvidar is a verb, olvido is a noun. You'll send her al olvido, the place where things are forgotten, so you can forget that you forgot them. Get it? Like that rumba callejera says—I forgot I had forgotten you.

Your boss at the welding shop will say nothing when you return to work. He'll have heard about your luck. He knows what it's like. He's been to Reno several times. Hard work at the welding shop is a satisfaction, the blue torch flame a soothing balm. Astral blue is the color of the hottest flame, and it melts the finest steel. You bend steel bars one at a time, that's all, you know exactly how, you know that's what the blue fire is for.

Time, in no hurry to go anywhere, will move real, real slow.

At the end of summer, her new CD, *Sex, Sexy, Sexo,* will be the talk of the town. The day you hear it you'll drive to Gilroy to hunt for garlic. Before leaving Gilroy you'll pay homage at the Holy Tree of the Virgen de Guadalupe in Pinto Lake County Park. The ancient oak where the Virgen miraculously appeared now turned into a shrine for the faithful who pray and leave photos, milagros, ribbons, and candles under the shady branches. Notes are pinned to the oak thanking the Virgen for her miracles—a life saved, a wandering lover who's returned, and so on. Even dollar bills are pressed into the sap between the bark. Silent before the Virgen, you'll fall on your knees with the rest of the faithful and meditate a while, trying to feel the beat of the cosmos, trying to hear the tin trumpets of angels. You'll ask the Virgen for a word, a sign. Some spiritual guidance.

But the image of the Virgen will not speak, she will perform no miracles for you. You'll hear only silence and the wind rustling leaves on the trees. You will feel how empty is the universe without the hope of seeing Lupita again. So you will take the gold medallion from your pocket, the one Lupita placed around your neck, the one she swore on, and you'll drape it from a branch of that old oak, an offering for the Virgen and the true believers. And you'll turn your back forever on religion and goddesses.

You'll lose track of the months and the seasons. You'll feel there's no purpose in life, like earthquakes and tsunamis have passed you by. And the future will mock you with dreams and hopes that belong to someone else.

Then one day without even knowing it you'll have peace with her memory. It will come to you without fanfare or lights or silver trumpets. Just a simple understanding of yourself. You can't ever erase her completely; she'll always be a scar, a stigmata, which, from time to time, will bleed a drop here and there. She'll forever be a part of you, good, bad, whatever. Your heart will tell you it was never meant to be; too much distance between her up on stage and you down in the welding shop. You'll realize you never did like conjunto music. You much prefer the driving rhythm of merengue, the sharp quick steps of salsa.

The next night at Polanco Gallery at an exhibit of wooden santos, while you sip wine and stare mindlessly out the window, beauty will skate by on roller blades wearing a baseball cap backwards, a walkman plugged to her ears and a fire-colored ponytail whipping in the wind. She'll be so unaware of her stunning good looks you'll crack a piropo in her honor, "Ay mamácita, si mujeres fueran fruta tú serias un mango."

And your one-armed heart, bruised and bloodied, will stir with life once more.

¡ZAS!

Printed in the USA
CPSIA information can be obtained
at www.ICGtesting.com
JSHW082211140824
68134JS00014B/564

9 780872 863941